Smolder

C.J.

SMOLDER

A Firefighters of Montana Romance

Happy reading!

Tracy Solheim

Tracy Solheim

TULE
PUBLISHING

CHAPTER ONE

A CHILLY EARLY morning breeze whispered off Flathead Lake, still icy in spots despite the calendar claiming it was springtime. Sam Gaskill cursed his stupidity for not buying a pair of gloves the minute he'd arrived in Glacier Creek. But the locals had all been walking around in shirt-sleeves the day before, citing the "balmy" Montana weather. And Sam couldn't afford to look weak. Not when he had so much to prove.

The lingering layer of snow crunched beneath his boots as he walked around the truck and opened the trailer door. Tabitha glanced over her shoulder, her big brown eyes seeming to plead with him.

"Yeah, I know, honey, we're not in Texas anymore." Sam blew on his hands and pulled his leather jacket more tightly around his neck. "But if you believe the weatherman, the snow should be gone in a day or two."

The mare stomped her foot with a snort. Sam smiled as he reached for the lead rope and attached it to her halter. "Yeah, I don't put much stock in the reliability of weather forecasters either." He ran his hand over the palomino's silky flank in order to sooth her. "But you're gonna like it here, girl. The pastures all border the lake. And the barn looks warm and comfortable."

Based upon his initial, quick inspection of the ranch, the state-of-the-art flagstone barn did look inviting—toasty and warm for both horses as well as humans. Despite the early morning hour, the twenty-stall stable was already bustling with activity. Sam heard the sounds of the horses grunting and nickering as their breakfast was being shoveled from a wheelbarrow into waiting feed buckets. A radio belted out a song in Spanish while a groom cheerfully whistled along with the tune. Sam breathed a sigh of relief, feeling better about his decision. If the condition of the facilities and the other horses were anything to go by, Tabitha would be well cared for at Whispering Breeze Ranch.

He unclipped the harness that secured her within the trailer stall. With a soft cluck and a gentle shove on her shoulder, Sam guided the horse backwards down the ramp. Her hooves were loud in the stable yard when they made contact with the metal. Once they'd reached the gravel drive, the good-natured mare lifted her nose in the air as if to assess her surroundings, her blonde mane lifting slightly with the breeze. She jerked her head suddenly at the sound of a low whistle.

"Well, I'll be damned. She sure is a beauty. Even prettier than her pictures." Clapping his hands together, Wayne Keenan, the rugged, middle-aged owner of Whispering

Breeze, strode from the barn. "I still can't believe my luck at having the only foal of the great Honey Bun and Honeysuckle boarding here. And she looks just like her mama." He pulled off a work glove and reverently stroked his fingers down the white blaze on Tabitha's face. The horse stood proudly, soaking in the attention. "You are a special girl, aren't you," Keenan murmured softly. "Bred to be a champion."

"She looks cold to me," a young voice said.

Sam turned toward the sliding barn doors where a young boy stood just inside. The child was dressed nearly identical to Keenan, wearing cowboy boots, jeans—baggy on his short, skinny legs—a shearling jacket, and a dark wool Sturgis Stetson that dipped low on his forehead. A black and white Boston terrier wiggled in his arms, yapping excitedly when Sam made eye-contact with it.

"You being the expert on animals that you are, Tyson, you're probably right." Keenan winked good-naturedly as he took the lead rope from Sam. "This pretty little filly can't be used to the cool mountain air. I'll take her inside and get her some breakfast, captain, while you settle up with the hauler."

Reluctantly, Sam let the rope slide through his fingers. He was doing what was best for the horse—honoring his late wife's dream. Still, he wondered if he was simply refusing to let go of the past.

Sam was starting over in a place far away from the plains of Texas and the mountains of Afghanistan. Hell, Montana might as well have been another planet. He didn't know a soul in Glacier Creek, and he liked it that way. After eleven months, he wouldn't be encountering pity in the eyes of everyone he met. He could take a breath of the cool mountain air and not taste guilt. But dragging the mare so far from home seemed both cruel and ridiculous. Yet leaving her behind had been unthinkable.

"Hey, mister." The little boy interrupted his thoughts. "Does your horse like peppermints?"

The trouble with living in a place where no one knew his story—or his deepest secrets—was that people kept getting the facts mixed up. Tabitha was not Sam's horse. She was, and always would be, Becky's. The mare had been Sam's gift to his wife weeks before his second deployment to the Middle East. In their first four years of marriage, he hadn't been able to give Becky a child. Instead, he'd given her a young horse to keep her company during his long absences. Five years later, the mare was all Sam had left of his wife.

"Yeah, she likes mints." Sam didn't bother correcting the boy. It didn't matter whose horse Tabitha was anymore. For all intents and purposes, she belonged to Wayne Keenan now. Sam was entrusting the renowned rancher with the care and training of his most precious possession. *His heartbreaking albatross.* "See that you don't spoil her breakfast, though."

The pint-sized cowboy continued to stare at him from beneath the brim of his hat until the dog scrambled out of his arms and began circling Sam's feet.

"Oreo doesn't like strangers," the boy declared.

Right on cue, Oreo began growling and lunging at Sam's boot. Reaching down, Sam grabbed the fifteen pounds of fur by the scruff of the neck and lifted the dog up so that they were nose to nose. Oreo's big licorice eyes grew even rounder as he squirmed beneath Sam's grip. Disciplining dogs wasn't any different from disciplining soldiers—or smokejumpers as he was now paid to do. It was all in the look and the tone of his voice. Sam had mastered both at a very young age. Growing up with a general for a father, he'd had to.

Sam glared at Oreo for a long moment until the terrier settled down with a whimper. "Behave," was all Sam said before handing the wee beastie off to its owner. Wrapping his arms around the dog, the boy turned on his heel and darted into the safety of the barn.

Great, now I'm scaring kids.

Sam shoved his fingers through his hair, longer today than it had been since he'd entered ROTC in college fourteen years earlier. Between his two sisters, he had five nieces and nephews, the younger two were likely close to the age of the boy who'd just hightailed it away from him. Sam used to be good with kids; the favorite uncle. But that was before war and death had changed him.

He didn't have time to worry about a child he'd likely rarely see, however. Once Tabitha was settled, Sam could focus on his new job overseeing the forest service station that served as a base to teams of smokejumpers and a search and rescue patrol. He'd be so busy keeping the fifty-some employees of the base in line that he wouldn't have time to check on the mare too often. That was why he'd selected Whispering Breeze for Tabitha. Keenan had agreed to train her so she was fit to be sold. He hoped her new owners would take the mare to compete in the American Quarter Horse Championship, Becky's dream for the horse. After that, Tabitha could happily live out her life with new owners as a brood mare. And Sam could move on. If that was even possible.

The driver of the horse trailer carried a hand-tooled, western saddle off the truck and placed it on top of the tack trunk he'd already unloaded. Sam pulled a check out of his wallet and handed it to the hauler. "Thanks for getting her here safely, Jimbo."

Jimbo adjusted the baseball cap on his head. "Your father-in-law thinks I took that horse to the glue factory months ago."

Sam felt his jaw grow tight. "It wasn't the horse's fault." He left the words about it being his own fault unsaid because he was pretty sure Jimbo knew that part. Hell, everyone in Belton, Texas, probably thought the same thing. Shaking off the memory, he clapped Jimbo on the shoulder and walked him to the driver's side of the truck. "I appreciate you keeping her for me."

"I did it for Becky." Jimbo's loyalty was clearly with his

late cousin who'd made the crazy decision to marry Sam when everyone else had told her not to. "You ever comin' back to Texas?"

Glancing up at the range of mountains looming behind the lake, their caps still covered in snow, Sam cleared the boulder from his throat. "Not much to come back to now."

Jimbo nodded mutely before climbing behind the wheel. His wife's cousin was no doubt relieved to see the last of Sam. "She never did like the idea of you hurling yourself out of perfectly good airplanes. Not that it matters much now. Still, you take care of yourself, Gaskill."

Sam shoved his cold hands into the pockets of his jeans as he watched Jimbo maneuver the horse trailer back onto the long drive leading to the highway. The guy was right—it didn't matter much what happened to Sam now. And if 'hurling himself out of perfectly good airplanes' chased away some of the numbness he felt, that was what he'd do. The fact that there'd be fire involved only made the jumps more challenging. And Sam needed something to challenge him— to thrill him—again.

"TRUMAN! NO!" LAUREL Keenan swatted at the kid goat trying to graze along the counter of her galley kitchen. She shoved Tyson's lunch into his backpack before her son's pet could destroy that, too. Grabbing Truman by his collar, she dragged him through the loft apartment she and Tyson shared.

Despite being housed above the stable, the space was cozy and modern thanks to her mother's talent as an interior designer. High ceilings lined with cherry wood complemented the bleached wood floors and the white stucco walls. The large living/dining area featured an iron chandelier that her mom had scavenged from an old boarding house near Butte. Laurel's airy bedroom was at one end of the nine-hundred-foot-space while Tyson's western themed bunk room was at the other end. The apartment was originally intended to be a guest house for visiting riders who came to Whispering Breeze to have their horses trained by Laurel's mother. But life had a way of messing up even the simplest of plans and now it was home to both Laurel and her son.

"Tyson Campbell Johnson," she called out as she hauled the goat, her son's backpack, and her coat down the stairs leading into the barn. "How many times have I told you that you have to keep the door closed so this damn nosy goat will keep his butt out of the loft?"

The familiar scent of leather, liniment, horse, and hay greeted her, along with a suspicious silence. Too bad for her son, the chilly morning air did nothing to cool off her annoyance. Aside from finding a goat nibbling at her breakfast, Tyson's father had texted saying he needed to speak with Laurel as soon as she'd dropped their son off at kindergarten. Both needed to happen before a very important meeting with her boss in just over an hour.

Oreo let out a little yip at the sight of the goat, but everyone else in the barn stood reverently admiring a gorgeous palomino horse munching on hay in one of the stalls—a palomino that had not been in that stall when Laurel had done the barn's night check eight hours earlier. Laurel none-too-gently shoved the goat toward the open barn door. "Where did that horse come from?"

Her father fiddled with the piece of straw in his mouth. "Isn't she a beauty?"

Apprehension fueled Laurel's annoyance. At twenty-eight, she could read her dad pretty accurately, and her father's words and demeanor told her he was up to something. "Yes, she is, but that wasn't the question I asked, Dad. *Where did she come from?*"

"She came from Texas," Tyson piped up.

"At seven-thirty in the morning? Did she walk here, then?" It was possible Laurel had missed the sound of a hauler while she was in the shower, but surely her father would have mentioned that he was expecting a horse to board with them; especially one as fine as the doe-eyed mare enjoying breakfast while an audience of worshipful men watched her every move like high school boys at a strip show. Laurel pulled on her puffy jacket to ward off the shivers brought on by both the morning chill and her premonition of trouble.

They hadn't kept many extra horses since her mother's health began failing nearly eight years ago. Before then, the

ranch had been home to many champion quarter horses her
mother had trained and Laurel had competed on. Today,
their stock consisted of hearty hacks her father used for
guided mountain tours and seasonal trail rides.

"She belongs to him." Tyson's mouth took on the familiar mulish look he got when she told the five-year-old he
couldn't buy candy at the grocery store checkout. Her sweet-
natured son was usually too friendly with strangers, so his
uncharacteristic animosity instantly put Laurel on guard.

She turned in the direction Tyson pointed. Her breath
caught in her lungs momentarily at the sight of the tall, well-
built man exiting the tack room. Amber eyes locked with
hers as he prowled toward the palomino, his boots deceptive-
ly silent on the stone floor for a man of his build.

His swagger identified him to Laurel instantly, however.
Her cousin's description of the new captain of Glacier
Creek's forest service station was dead on—broad shoulders,
wavy dark hair, perpetual five o'clock shadow, and an
arrogant chin. Miranda had left out one crucial detail,
though. The guy had a most exceptional ass. Laurel swallowed roughly when he walked past her to pat the horse on
its withers.

The new station captain was definitely perpetuating the
tough guy persona he'd ridden into town with a week ago.
His light leather bomber jacket and well-worn Levis weren't
much of a defense against the crisp morning air in the
flatlands. But if he wasn't complaining, she'd just enjoy the

view.

"Laurel, this is Captain Gaskill," her father said. "An actual captain, as a matter of fact. He just left the army. Those boys over at the forest service base won't know how to act with a real soldier commanding them."

She grimaced at her father's uncharacteristic tactlessness. Russ Edwards, the station's previous captain, died tragically seven months ago when his parachute clipped a tree during a fire jump. The smokejumpers—as well as most of the town—had taken Russ's death hard. Laurel's uncle, Hugh Ferguson, had stepped back into his old job of station captain while the forest service recruited a new commander for the base, but most of the young smokejumpers only knew Hugh as the bartender from their favorite watering hole, The Drop Zone.

Needless to say, discipline and morale had been lacking during the off-season. Two of Laurel's cousins worked at the station, so she knew the crews all deeply resented the forest service hiring someone from the outside. From what she'd heard, the army captain had his work cut out for him. Laurel almost felt sorry for him.

"And this here"—her father gestured to the mare—"is Tupelo Honey, the foal of Honey Bun and Honeysuckle. She goes by Tabitha in the barn. The captain is going to keep her at the ranch while he's in Glacier Creek. Aren't we lucky?"

Laurel didn't see anything lucky about the arrangement.

Her spidey-sense was still telling her there was more to the story.

She let her gaze wander back to the sexy ex-soldier. "So, you ride, captain?"

Sam Gaskill's chin never moved while his arresting eyes slowly checked out Laurel from head to toe. Pulling her coat more tightly around her, she tried not to let the sensation of being given the once over by a lion scouting out his prey unnerve her. Instead she squared her chin and met the captain's assessing gaze head on. *So much for feeling sorry for the guy.*

His lips barely moved. "I don't."

"Yet, you own a champion-bred quarter horse?"

"She belonged to my wife." This time his mouth grew harder, if that was even possible.

"Oh, well, there's your first mistake. You should have bought her some jewelry or a car so when you split it up you wouldn't be stuck with something so difficult to pawn."

He stiffened at her flippant remark and her father let out a beleaguered groan.

"My *late* wife." The three words crackled through the frosty air and Laurel felt each one like a slap to the face.

She didn't bother looking at her dad, who was likely wearing that pained look he always did when she spoke without thinking. Would she never learn? Her mother claimed Laurel had been born without the essential filter that ran from her brain to her mouth. Needless to say, impulsiveness had been Laurel's downfall on more than one occasion.

Her cheeks were hot and her palms sweaty as she pushed the words out of her mouth. "Forgive me. That was beyond rude."

A charged silence hovered within the barn as the oblivious mare continued to chew on hay. Laurel forced herself to meet the captain's eyes. She was surprised to see the pain that was reflected there before he quickly extinguished it. Her stomach quivered in embarrassment.

"I've got to get to work," he said stoically before running a hand along the mare's sleek back. The intimate gesture brought out an unexpected flush to more than just Laurel's face.

"Take good care of her. Let me know if you need anything else for her training." His footsteps sounded much more commanding in retreat, and it wasn't until Laurel heard the hum of his vehicle making its way along the drive that his last words registered.

"Training? What kind of training was he talking about, Dad?"

Her father shot her a disapproving look, likely left over from when she'd put her foot in her mouth moments earlier. But Laurel refused to let it deter her.

"You did tell the guy that Mom hasn't trained a horse in years, didn't you? He knows that she's in a wheelchair and doesn't ride anymore, right, Dad?"

Her father shoved his hat back on his head and squeezed

at his temple. "I'm not some snake oil salesman, Laurel. Of course I told him all that."

Laurel slapped her hands on her denim-clad thighs in exasperation. "Then why did you tell him we were going to train his horse?"

"Because we are!" His bellowed words echoed off the stone walls, startling the mare and sending the grooms scurrying back to work. Tyson looked on wide-eyed while Oreo let out a whimper.

Laurel felt as though the barn was spinning. "Who do you mean when you say 'we'?" Although, she had a sinking feeling she already knew the answer to her question.

"You!" Her father pulled his hat off his head and dragged his long fingers through his shaggy silver hair. "I mean you, Laurel."

Staggering back a step, she nearly tripped over Tyson's backpack. "You can't be serious? I don't know the first thing about training a horse. That's Mom's talent. I just ride them. What possibly made you think I could—*or would*—do it?"

"For crying out loud, Laurel, the man's wife is dead." His voice trailed off as he stared past the barn door toward the house across the gravel drive where her mother likely waited to share breakfast with him. The barn was tense and quiet for a moment before her father swallowed fiercely, his fingers tightening on the brim of his hat. "She'd raised the horse from a foal and it was her dream to see it compete at the highest level."

The captain's wife had been a horsewoman like her mother then. That familiar fear that always gripped her when she thought of her mother dying added to the anxiety that already had Laurel on edge. Josephine Keenan had always been larger than life. Not only was she a popular designer for many of the stars who had vacation homes in the region, but her mother had served as the town's elected mayor for eight years. She was a vibrant fixture in Glacier Creek until fate had intervened. Her mom's multiple sclerosis was stable, her prognosis cautiously optimistic, but Laurel knew how quickly circumstances—and life—could change. From the looks of it, so did her father.

"Tyson." She pushed out around the tightening in her chest. "Take Oreo up to the house and say good morning to your grandma. I'll be up in a minute to drive you to school." She reached down and handed her son his backpack. Tyson eyed his grandfather before wisely slipping out of the barn. Truman fell into step behind him.

"Is there something you're not telling me, Dad," she asked as soon as Tyson and his menagerie had cleared the door. "Something about Mom?"

Her father swore under his breath. "No, of course not."

"Then why would you commit me to training a man's horse?

"The captain's wife already trained the damn horse, Laurel. You're welcome to watch the videos." He reached out and patted the horse's neck. "She just needs some fine tuning so he can sell the animal. Two, maybe three months at the max."

"Two to three months?" Laurel gasped. "Dad, even if I thought I knew how to 'tune up' a horse to the caliber this one needs to be, where am I going to find the time? I work full-time. I help out here at the ranch, and I'm studying for my CPA, remember?"

Her father finally turned so his brown eyes met hers head-on. Her breath caught at the vulnerability she saw in them. "I already hired an extra hand to help out on the trail rides and the overnights so you'd have more time to study. He starts next week."

His words surprised her. Up until now, he'd been dismissive regarding her ability to become an accountant. Laurel was the first to agree the career didn't naturally fit with her personality, but she was quick with numbers and the work provided an adequate challenge for her impulsive brain. Not only that, but she had a son to support—without her parents' help. Unfortunately, her father's opinion led to a great deal of self-doubt on her own part. His willingness to help her out now, in spite of the motivation behind that support, wasn't something she could easily dismiss.

"The days are getting longer," he continued. "I thought that maybe you could work with the horse in the evenings. Your mom could come out and watch while it's still warm from the sun. It could be just like old times; her coaching you from the rail." His voice broke slightly and Laurel felt it reverberate deep within her chest cavity. "I don't think the captain is expecting miracles, honey. But I know both he and your mother would get something from it. The man was deployed in a war zone three times. He deserves our respect and whatever help we can give. And your mom. . .well, she deserves something to look forward to every day."

Laurel didn't know how to respond to her father. The morning had been a tsunami of anxious emotions already and she wasn't sure how she felt about anything. She opened her mouth to say what, she had no idea, when Tyson came charging back into the barn.

"Mom, the big hand is on the twelve and the little hand is on the eight. We need to get to school. Miss Ivy said she'd let me turn on the computers and iPads today!"

Her father cleared his throat before putting his hat back on his head. "Well then, we'd better get you loaded up into your car seat. We don't want Miss Ivy giving your special job to anyone else." He gave Laurel's arm a squeeze as he passed her. "Just think about it, Laurel. For once, give the situation time to settle before you react."

He followed Tyson out of the barn, leaving her alone with the mare and enough guilt to swallow her whole. The horse eyed Laurel warily as she approached.

"You are a looker, I'll give you that," she said softly while the mare continued to crunch on her hay. Laurel pulled a mint out of her coat pocket and let it rest in her flat palm. The palomino hesitated coyly before sniffing Laurel's fingers and finally taking the mint with a lick of her hand. Releasing a resigned sigh, Laurel patted the horse's nose. "We'll just take it one day at a time and see what happens."

The horn on her beat-up Land Cruiser sounded as she gave the mare a final pat. "Gotta go. Tyson loves school and it makes him impatient in the mornings. Boys can be such a pain." The horse snorted. "Your guy, too, huh?" Laurel said, sarcastically. "Hmm, I never would have guessed." With a quick check to see if the stall door was secure, Laurel headed out of the barn to get on with her already crazy day.

CHAPTER TWO

S AM LET HIS legs dangle off the jump tower as he carefully took in the scene a hundred feet beneath his boots. A
group of ten men and women were scrambling around on
the ground below, hauling parachutes and pulaskis from one
side of the damp field to the other. The afternoon sun had
warmed up the day substantially and most of the crew was in
short sleeves while carrying out routine training drills.

Nestled a couple of hundred yards east of Flathead Lake
and backing up to two point three million acres of the
Flathead National Forest, the Glacier Creek forest service
station was a twenty-acre facility housing two airplane
hangars, a helipad, and a seven-thousand-square-foot log
cabin. The cabin included not only the main offices of the
service, but a large assembly room, a small workout area, and
a kitchen, as well as a bunk house for on-call staff. Two large
equipment sheds stood behind the cabin, storing the tools of
the trade for the crews that worked out of the station. A
gravel parking lot separated the main building from the two-
hundred-fifty-foot jump tower and the vast open field below
it known as Dead Man's Valley—a place where rookies were

either made or broken each spring.

"I have to admit, I was a little leery of your idea for a mini-boot camp, but I guess it's better if they try to kill themselves out here rather than inside the station." Vincent Kingston, one of the eighteen year-round employees, sat down on the platform beside Sam. Mud was caked along his tattooed arm and the knees of his cargo pants, but Kingston wore it like a badge of honor, having bested two hotshots in a fire line drill moments earlier.

"Ferguson's singing while he sewed up parachutes this morning wasn't conducive to getting any paperwork done," Sam said.

The tension inside the station was fueled not only by having a new leader from outside the ranks, but also by the competitive nature of the permanent employees who manned the base. Most of the men and women working year-round were team leaders who would command the part-time employees due to arrive for boot camp in a few weeks. Those who'd spent the winter in the station were getting antsy for some action. Testing and cleaning equipment—not to mention repairing parachutes—had become tedious to a group of individuals used to performing arduous physical activities for months at a time. They needed something to blow off steam before they blew up at each other. Hence the unscheduled afternoon boot camp.

Kingston laughed at the remark about the smokejumper's singing. "Liam's voice has a very different effect on the women in his father's bar. I've seen them throw their panties at him during karaoke night."

"Remind me to avoid The Drop Zone on karaoke night then." Glancing out of the corner of his eye, Sam studied the man next to him. He wasn't surprised that Kingston had out-maneuvered the other firefighters at the drill; the guy clearly possessed the stamina and intelligence to be a first rate smokejumper/hotshot. In the seven days since Sam had taken over the station, he'd watched the other employees take their cues from the steely man. It was obvious to him that the rest of the crew had assumed either Kingston or Tyler Dodson might be their new captain rather than an outsider like Sam.

Kingston had been Russ Edwards' best friend—he even lived in Edwards' old house and brought the former captain's dog, Muttley, to the station every day. But Sam sensed that behind the intensity, Kingston wasn't exactly settled in his own skin. According to the file on the incident that left Edwards dead, Kingston was the first to arrive on the scene, finding his friend unconscious, dangling from his chute. Edwards never awoke before succumbing to internal injuries. It was a scenario Sam could relate to, having lived it more than once during his tours of duty in the army. But he, like Kingston, knew the risks involved with the job. Losing a friend, while not easy, was chief among those risks.

The chilly welcome Sam had received when he took over as captain hadn't warmed one bit. Sam knew having Kingston's support would go a long way to winning over the rest of the crew. He didn't give a rat's ass whether anyone in the station actually liked him, but he needed their respect to ensure things ran efficiently—and safely—this fire season. That was job one. Sam hadn't botched a mission yet—his marriage, well, that was another story.

"I'm almost finished going over the applications for rookie candidates and the returning part-time jumpers," Sam said. "We're going to have to cast the net a little wider to make sure that, for boot camp, we have at least a dozen applicants who have significant emergency medical training. Right now, only thirty percent of our personnel are EMT qualified. That's not enough to make sure each jump crew will have personnel with advanced medical training. I want to double that number."

Kingston's body went very still as even his breathing seemed to halt for a long moment. Sam had been right to guess the guy was carrying around a load of unnecessary guilt over his friend's death. But until they were actually facing down a fire, he had no way of knowing whether or not Kingston had lost his edge. His gut was telling him the guy was one of the strongest leaders in the station. Sam was counting on the fact Kingston still had the mettle to do the job. The broadening of specialized EMT experience to each team was Sam's way of allowing every crew member to face the fire season after their captain's death with a little less guilt—particularly the man sitting beside him.

"We'll add a more comprehensive first-aid training unit that's beyond what the forest service requires to the boot camp. But it will be mandatory for every member of the crew, regardless of their experience," Sam continued. "I've arranged for a combat medic I know to come and give the course early next month."

With a whoosh of a breath, Kingston gave him a slow, deliberate nod.

"Dodson is helping me understand the nuances of coordinating among the local, regional, and national agencies. I'm also going to need some help assessing the skill-set of the returning seasonal crew. Is that something you feel comfortable doing?" Sam asked. "Next to Dodson, you have the most seniority and are familiar with the part-time personnel."

Kingston turned and eyed him shrewdly. If he suspected Sam's motive, he kept it to himself. "So no one's guaranteed a job? A lot of people in this area are counting on that income for the summer."

"Everyone's got a job." Kingston nodded as Sam continued. "But there's a lot more to an individual than what is on their application, and I don't have the luxury of getting up to speed on everyone before the fire season starts. I'm hoping you can help me put together the most efficient crews using more information than what is in their files. Provided I can even find their files. It doesn't look like any paperwork has been completed around here in months."

Kingston gave him a sheepish look before glancing back down below his sneakers. "That's because Hugh Ferguson refused to replace Jacqui. Edwards' wife was the office manager for the station. She started working here as a volunteer intern when she was just a teenager and then took a permanent G-S job when she graduated high school. She basically ran the place ever since."

Sam knew Russ Edwards' wife was currently on leave without pay from the forest service. But with the fire season fast approaching and the addition of thirty seasonal employees—all of whom needed to be paid—he couldn't afford to be without a permanent office manager.

"I take it she doesn't plan to return to work?"

"She hasn't stepped foot in the station since Russ died. She left for Florida right after the funeral. She's headed back for a couple of days to deal with some issues that have cropped up with their—*her*—house."

"Any chance you could convince her to let me buy her a cup of coffee? I'd like to get her position with the service resolved so we can move ahead."

Kingston's jaw tensed for some unknown reason, making Sam think there was more to the situation. All he was concerned with right now, however, was making sure things at the station were running smoothly before all hell broke loose.

"I'll mention it to her." Kingston shot Sam a frosty glance. "But I won't have her upset while she's here. Is that clear?"

So there was more to the story. Not that it was any of his business. Sam didn't back down from Kingston's stare. "Just coffee and boring government files. The worst that could happen is a paper cut."

"Sure." Kingston conceded after a long moment. He then retrained his eyes to the scene below them where Liam Ferguson was taking on two other crew members in a drill that had them crawling on their bellies through a rope obstacle.

"What's the four-one-one on Ferguson?" Sam asked.

Kingston relaxed beside him. "Despite the devil-may-care personality, he's one hell of a firefighter. It's in the genes. He spent the last couple of years in Australia working with crews in Queensland and Sydney; just got back to the States six weeks ago. He'll tell you he went for the adventure, but I suspect it was because he wanted to earn his own reputation. Both his brothers jump with the crew out of Redlands, California. His father was captain here for fifteen years before Russ took the helm."

"So he wasn't around last fall."

Kingston swallowed roughly, but Sam knew that the other man understood what he was getting at. Liam Ferguson hadn't been on the jump when Russ Edwards had died. That meant he likely wasn't harboring the guilt that the man sitting beside him was.

"No."

"I'd like for him to head up a crew then."

"Will you be jumping? It's not technically part of your job description."

Sam turned to look at Kingston. "I won't send a man or woman into a fire that I wouldn't jump into myself. It doesn't have to be in my job description. It's in my blood."

A slight smile—one that looked touched with admiration—crossed Kingston's face. "Russ used to say the same thing. His motto was 'One ass to risk', meaning he wasn't going to risk anyone else's ass before he'd risk his own."

So that's what that is on his chute. The late captain's parachute hung in memoriam inside the station. It was draped reverently from the second story loft so everyone entering the building would see it. To those who gazed upon it, the memorial was a daily reminder of the friend they'd lost. To Sam, it was a constant sign that he had a long way to go towards earning the trust of the men and women who had served under Edwards.

"I'd like both you and Dodson to take a major role in assessing the rookies," Sam said. "Let me know if there's anyone else you think might make a good team leader."

Kingston seemed to search the field with his eyes before settling on a dark-haired man leaning up against the hood of a pickup truck on the outer edge of the parking lot. "That guy," Kingston said, gesturing with his chin. "Ace Clark."

As far as Sam could tell, Clark was a bit of a wiseass who seemed the most resentful of Sam's presence at the station.

The guy didn't appear to take too many things seriously, especially the few assignments Sam had doled out since arriving. The fact that he chose to ignore the mini-boot camp this afternoon spoke volumes to Sam about Clark's commitment. Or lack thereof.

Kingston seemed to sense his reticence. "Don't be so quick to judge. The kid has had a pretty hard life. But he's more capable than he appears. He's one of the first guys I'd pick to have my back in a fire."

Sam studied Clark, who seemed to be good-naturedly heckling his coworkers as they navigated the course. His gut usually never let him down, but he couldn't get a good read on the young firefighter.

"Trust is a two-way street, captain," Kingston said from beside him. "You may need to give a little to get some back in return. You asked for my opinion and that—along with Clark being a solid asset—is my two cents."

The sun dipped lower, warming Sam's face as the men and women below laughingly made their way toward the station, presumably to shower and head home. He was responsible for the lives of all of the people below him—along with a couple of dozen arriving next month. It was against his nature to leave anything to luck, much less trust. But if he was going to count on Vincent Kingston to jump into a fire, Sam needed to trust Kingston's judgment, too. All he could do was pray they both weren't making a mistake.

"All right," he said with a nod. "We'll give Clark a chance. I'll jump with his team the first time out and see how it goes."

"Looks like everyone survived field day without killing each other. I think that calls for some nachos and a cold one," Kingston said as he got to his feet. "I'm just gonna jump in the shower before heading over to The Drop Zone. Care to join me for a beer? I'm buying."

"That depends. It isn't karaoke night, is it?"

Kingston shook his head. "Even better; it's half-price burger night."

"In that case, count me in."

"I'll meet you there in half an hour." Kingston climbed down the metal ladder. The sound of Muttley's barking grew more excited as he got closer to the ground.

Sam glanced over toward the forest service station where some of the crew members were already making their way home. As dusk began to settle over the area, Sam's new home away from home was bathed in pink sunlight that reflected off the many windows circling the second floor of the massive log cabin. A flock of geese landed on the lake with a loud flurry of wings and excited honking.

This day had been Sam's best so far since arriving in Montana. Kingston was right; while the morale within the staff hadn't improved, it hadn't gotten any worse and that was a win in Sam's book. Easing his mind even more, Tabitha was safely ensconced at the Whispering Breeze

Ranch.

Sam fixed his gaze across the horizon. Squinting against the sun's glare on the lake, he could just make out the stone barn where the mare was likely enjoying her dinner. Muttley barked excitedly, making Sam wonder about the little dog, Oreo, and the boy who'd been in the stable this morning. His mind immediately made a beeline to the young boy's insufferable mother. Wayne Keenan's daughter might be a world champion rider, but she was a callous, spoiled little rich girl, too.

She was also sexy as hell.

Sam hadn't been able to get the image of her sassy mouth out of his head all day. It was one of the reasons he'd insisted on some unplanned, outdoor calisthenics. He'd hoped the cool air would chill the parts of him that kept thinking about the arrogant woman's long legs wrapped around more than just a horse.

He couldn't understand why he was attracted to her at all. She was nothing like Becky. His wife had been demure and genteel with sun-kissed blonde hair and eyes that were as blue as Texas bluebells. Laurel Keenan walked around as though she owned the world, her pert little nose up in the air, her green eyes glowing with attitude, while she tossed her long brown hair around like a pulaski. His mind drifted back to her mouth again, and what he wanted her to do with it made his jeans grow unbearably tight.

Sam quickly jumped up. He needed that beer more than

he thought. Guilt nipped at him at the carnal images that had been wracking his body all day. It was just lust. He'd been celibate so long he'd feel this way about any attractive woman who crossed his path—even one with a young child and who was likely happily married.

He needed something to occupy his body and his thoughts that was all. But fire season was still nearly two months off. Right now, even karaoke night with women tossing their thong underwear at Liam Ferguson sounded like a good idea. As long as it distracted Sam's mind from the woman caring for his horse.

"I'M SORRY. DID you just say Bryce is getting *married?*" Miranda Ferguson's shocked voice rose above the din coming from the crowd within The Drop Zone. The sound of pool balls ricocheting off one another warred with the noise from random sporting events blaring from the televisions mounted on the walls.

The Drop Zone was a landmark in Glacier Creek. The long, narrow room featured a smattering of twenty round dining tables, a fifty-foot carved oak bar rescued from an old brothel in the mining town of Taft, and tin ceilings with scenes of the gold rush imprinted on the tiles. Two pool tables occupied the back of the bar where a vintage jukebox wailed next to a small dance floor. Laurel's uncle, Hugh Ferguson, and two of his hotshot cronies had bought The

Drop Zone nearly fifteen years ago, saving it from demolition and turning it into a favorite dining spot for locals.

"Shhh!" Laurel pleaded with her cousin as she glanced at the tables around them to see if the other patrons had overheard. "I'd rather word didn't get out just yet."

"Are you worried this will blow your cover story that Bryce is gay and that's why he hasn't married you?" their waitress asked as she placed a trio of drinks on the table. "Because really, anyone with access to *TMZ* has known for years that was a lie."

Crossing her arms over her chest, Laurel leaned back in her chair and glared at Tori Kingston. Tori responded with a cheeky grin before strutting off in her cute boots and tight jeans to flirt with a table of suits from the local insurance company.

"Ignore her," Ivy Harris said from beside Laurel. "Seriously, the best thing Vin Kingston did was come to his senses and divorce that woman."

Miranda fiddled with the bottle of beer in front of her. "Ivy's right, Tori has always been jealous of you. But she does have a point. Bryce Johnson getting married is going to be big news, even if his bride-to-be wasn't a Dutch model. It's going to be hard to keep something like this quiet."

Laurel gave her friends a resigned nod. Tyson's father was an internationally famous snowboarder with the reputation of being a daredevil who played as hard off the slopes as he did on them. His feats were fodder not only for the record books, but the tabloids as well.

"Bryce and Audrianna aren't planning to announce their engagement until they tell Tyson." Laurel swallowed painfully as she slumped down in her chair. "Bryce wants to tell him in person during their trip to Disneyland next week."

Reaching for her glass of chardonnay with a less than steady hand, she took a fortifying sip. She could barely afford to take her son to Chuck-E-Cheese, much less Disneyland. It was killing her to miss her son's first meet and greet with Mickey Mouse.

Bryce was extremely generous with his child support, but Laurel was careful to spend it only on the essentials for their son. The rest she invested cautiously, not wanting to take the chance that Tyson's father wouldn't blow his fortune. *Or break his neck.* One of them had to be the sensible grown-up and look out for Tyson's future. Laurel was just as surprised as the next person that she'd turned out to be the responsible one.

Ivy patted her on the shoulder. "How do you think Tyson will take the news?"

"Probably better than he would if the kid heard *you* were getting married." Miranda joked.

Laurel bit back her first real grin of the day. Ivy was Tyson's kindergarten teacher. Her son had always had a crush on his mother's childhood friend, but once he'd landed in Ivy's classroom, his crush had morphed into worshipful adulation.

"Well, Tyson needn't worry. There's no chance of that happening anytime soon." Ivy took a healthy swallow from her appletini while her eyes drifted across the room to where Liam Ferguson sat joking with several of the smokejumpers from the forest service station. Tyson wasn't the only one in Laurel's orbit with an unrequited love.

Laurel exchanged a look with her cousin. Miranda rolled her eyes in exasperation, evidently unable to understand what any sane woman would see in her twin brother. Tori returned with their spinach dip and tortilla chips.

"The word is you're going to be back on the circuit again, Laurel," the waitress said. "Has it really been ten years since you stood in this very bar, fresh off being crowned the AQHA world champion in reining horses, and declared you'd never put on a pair of spurs again? I guess all those dreams of making it big somewhere outside of Montana never really came true, huh? Well, they do say it's best to stick with what you know. Especially when everything else fails."

Laurel did her best to tamp down on the anger and humiliation brought on by Tori's words. Beside her, Ivy choked on her drink. Uncle Hugh, still quick on his feet, was pressing his daughter back down into her chair before Laurel realized Miranda had stood to defend her.

"Tori," her uncle barked. "You've got orders up. Don't keep the customers waiting."

The waitress sashayed away without so much as an apology. Not that she needed to apologize. Everything she'd said had been the truth. Laurel sighed. She'd had big plans once. Plans that took her away from Glacier Creek to some place exciting and different. Any place. Truth be told, she was once as reckless and daring as Bryce Johnson, craving excitement and a life that was dramatically different than the one she was now living.

But then reality hit in the form of an unplanned pregnancy and a sick mother. Laurel left school, returning home to the ranch and her old life with barely a thought of what might have been. The impulsive dreamer inside her had been snuffed out by the pragmatic realist circumstances had created. Growing up quickly had been painful, but Laurel had survived it and she had the bonus of a lovable young son to ease the transition. She wouldn't trade Tyson—or these past years with her ailing mother—for any adventure in the world.

"Don't mind her. Tori's been a bit ornery since the divorce," Uncle Hugh was saying. "Most of the customers love her and she does a good job. Still, I'll have a talk with her."

Laurel waved her uncle off. "It's okay, Uncle Hugh. She's just saying what everyone in town is thinking."

Her uncle's blue eyes sparkled with compassion and a hint of pity as he headed back to the bar.

"Nobody's mind works like Tori's," Miranda said, her voice laced with loathing.

"Yeah. And no one thinks you're a failure, either," Ivy

insisted. "Just wait until you pass your CPA exam and Rusty gives you the job as chief accountant. Besides, I thought you were just training the captain's horse, not actually competing on it?"

"Wait, what?" Miranda paused with her chip mid-scoop to glance between Ivy and Laurel. "You're riding again? And what captain are you talking about?"

"Your captain," Ivy said before digging into the dip herself. "You missed some important gossip today while you were flying mint over to Billings."

Miranda worked as a commercial pilot. When she wasn't shuttling smokejumpers to and from fires or conducting search and rescue operations for the forest service, she was hauling cargo from the farms and small manufacturing plants within the region. Today her shipment had been mint from one of the state's last remaining mint farms. The same farm where Laurel worked as a bookkeeper.

"At least her plane smells a lot better today than it does during fire season." Uncle Hugh winked at his daughter as he placed their burgers on the table.

"Will somebody catch me up here," Miranda said. "I didn't know the captain had a horse."

"Technically it's his wife's horse." Laurel groaned as she remembered her ugly faux pas from earlier in the day. "His *late* wife's horse."

"He brought a horse with him? A horse that isn't even his?" Miranda asked.

Ivy dragged a French fry through the ketchup on her plate. "He couldn't bear to part with it. It's so romantic."

"Kind of creepy if you ask me," Miranda said. "So, I take it he's boarding it at your place. And you're competing on it?"

"Not competing on it. Just training her." Laurel hadn't given her father a definitive answer yet, but it looked like she was well and truly stuck with the task now that the gossip had reached The Drop Zone. "It was apparently his late wife's wish that the horse compete nationally. The least I can do is to get the mare ready for that. The guy did serve his country—three times," she said, parroting her father's argument from the morning. "Besides, romantic or not, who could say no with those eyes of his piercing through you. And it's partially your fault I got into this anyway, Miranda. You might have mentioned that a woman should have at least two cups of coffee before catching a glimpse of the guy's sexy ass."

Laurel looked up from her burger to see both her friends staring at her. "What?"

"Interesting," was all Miranda said. Ivy grinned mischievously.

Laurel scoffed at her friends. "It's not what you think. Besides, I was pretty rude to him this morning. I'm sure he thinks I'm an idiot."

"Hmm, that is interesting." Ivy's smile grew wider. "You rarely lose your cool anymore. In fact, you keep your emotions on a pretty tight leash. I wonder what could have set you off this morning?" She rested her chin in her palm. "Pheromones would be my guess. You did say something about him being sexy."

"Stop it, both of you," Laurel demanded. "I was rude to the man because I was stressed out by Bryce's text, not because I was flustered or attracted to him." The flush she felt burning her cheeks was likely calling her out as a liar. "It's a wonder he even left his horse at the ranch, given the way I spoke to him."

"You should probably go over to his table and apologize then."

Laurel's breath left her body in a whoosh. "He's here?"

Miranda smirked at her. "'Sexy ass' and all. And he can't take his eyes off you. They've been burning a hole into the back of your head for the last five minutes. I'm surprised my dad hasn't pulled out the fire extinguisher by now."

Before she could tell her body not to, Laurel glanced over her shoulder. Sure enough, there was Captain Cowboy seated at a table in the far corner of the bar, nonchalantly leaning the back of his chair against a section of wall featuring a poster that read—*Forget the truck, ride a firefighter*. He paused in the act of taking a sip from his longneck bottle of beer to lock eyes with her. The look he gave her was hot and hard. She spun back around to see Ivy fanning herself with her napkin while Miranda laughed out loud.

Laurel took a gulp of her wine, but it did nothing to cool

the heat rising within her. "You're being ridiculous." The words were meant for her friends as much as herself. The man was arrogant and bold beyond words. He was probably as used to women throwing themselves at him as her cousin Liam was.

"Oh, mercy. My panties are wet and I wasn't even the target of that 'do me' look," Ivy said.

"That was *not* a 'do me' look," Laurel hissed. "That was a 'turn around and stop stalking me' glare. I told you, he thinks I'm a nut case." She dropped her head into her hands. "Hell, *I* think I'm a nut case."

"Why? Because you're attracted to a hot, rugged guy?" Miranda asked. "It's about time. You've been behaving like a nun for the past five years. There's no crime in talking to the guy to see where things go. I mean, I would if he wasn't practically my boss. Even Ivy here would if she wasn't so hung up on my goofy brother."

"Definitely," Ivy conceded as she bobbed her blonde head solemnly.

Laurel stared at her two friends. "I haven't been acting like a nun" she protested.

"Sex toys don't count," Miranda interjected.

"I have been protecting my son's reputation. And I don't want to give people in this town more to gossip about."

"The only thing they're gossiping about is whether or not you're still waiting around for Bryce to come to his senses," Miranda said softly. "And now he's getting married.

You need to move on, too."

Laurel felt as if she might shatter with her next breath. Had everyone been thinking she was pining for Bryce? Well, she hadn't been. Theirs was a short-lived affair during a summer she'd spent waitressing at a resort in Lake Tahoe. She liked and even respected him, but all she'd ever felt for him was infatuation. Certainly not like the love she felt for their son. Laurel hadn't *moved on* because she hadn't met anyone worth *moving on* to.

Her friends were right, though; she hadn't really been looking for that guy. Not that Captain Cowboy was *that guy*. He was a bit too insufferable—not to mention way too sexy. But she did owe him an apology for her inelegant words that morning. After all, if she'd be training his horse—*his wife's horse*—it would be nice if they could be friends.

"I'm going over there to mend a professional relationship that got off on the wrong foot, nothing more," she said as she stood up, not giving her friends the time to challenge her words. But when she turned around, he was gone. She swung forward just in time to see his sexy ass retreating out The Drop Zone's front door.

CHAPTER THREE

T HE QUIET OF the barn was soothing following the rowdy
atmosphere of the bar. Sam stood outside Tabitha's stall
listening to the hushed sounds of the horses dozing on their
feet, punctuated occasionally by a snort and the rustle of
shavings when one of them shifted position. The night air
smelled clean and brisk, portending another chilly morning
ahead, but the barn was snug and warm, just as Sam knew it
would be. He should have just gone back to the small A-
frame cabin he'd rented and unpacked the last few boxes—
one of which likely contained his pair of gloves. Instead, he'd
steered his truck toward the Whispering Breeze Ranch. He
told himself he was only doing so to check on the mare.

Of course, he knew he was lying. Hell, even Tabitha likely knew it. A burger and a cold beer had done nothing to
ease the restlessness that Wayne Keenan's daughter had
ignited within Sam's long dormant libido. Seeing her at The
Drop Zone had only made the problem worse. The un-
touchable vibe she gave off kept most of the male population
in the bar from approaching her, but for Sam, her demeanor
was like a red flag to a charging bull.

And he didn't like the feeling one bit.

Sam had come to Montana to shake off the torrent of emotions that had been dogging him these past months, not to stir up new ones. He was generally a pretty even-tempered guy—cool under fire. The ability to keep his emotions under wraps was something he'd been known for throughout his military career. Of course, with everything that had gone on in his life the past year, he wasn't as cool as he'd like to be. Tonight, he'd gone to the barn figuring that reconnecting with the one thing his late wife loved most would quell whatever was brewing inside of him.

So far, it wasn't working.

Tabitha nuzzled Sam's outstretched hand, presumably looking for a treat. When she found none, she turned a shoulder to him and let her eyelids drift shut. Sam wondered if the mare missed Becky; whether she, too, blamed him for taking her away. That familiar squeezing was back in his chest.

"Well, you can just get in line to hate me with everybody else," he admonished the horse.

"You're not a'pposed to be in here," a voice said behind him, startling Sam.

He turned to find the little boy—Tyson—who'd been in the barn this morning. The boy was standing on a set of stairs that presumably led to a living area above. He was wearing a pair of Star Wars stormtrooper pajamas and red cowboy boots. His blue eyes were large against his rosy cheeks and damp, wavy brown hair. The tough guy expression he was trying to work his mouth into lost a lot of potency when Sam glanced down at the ragged stuffed animal Tyson had clutched against his chest.

"And I'm pretty sure you're supposed to be in bed," Sam said.

Tyson's chin jutted up as he stomped down the two remaining steps. The sound of his boots hitting the stone floor made a few of the horses stir. "I'm not some baby who goes to bed early. I have chores. I'm doing the night check." He marched along the aisle, going from stall door to stall door, testing every latch to see if it was secure, all the while softly calling out a goodnight to the individual horses inside. Sam had to admire the boy's pluck as he mimicked a drill he'd probably seen his grandfather or one of his parents perform many times before.

The boy stopped abruptly at a stall across from Tabitha's and began fumbling with the lock. "What's wrong, Tator Tot?" he asked as he tried and failed to get the stall door open. He pulled harder before turning to Sam with a desperate look on his face. "Can you help me, mister?"

Suddenly Sam was furious at Laurel and her husband for neglecting their son, leaving him unsupervised in a barn where anything could happen. He thought of the child Becky took with her to the grave and his anger grew. Sam reached for the latch just as Tyson had worked it open.

"You're not going in there," he told the boy. It was one

thing to let Tyson play like he was an adult, but to whatever animal was inside that stall, he'd be a defenseless child.

Tyson's lip began to quiver. "But I gotta make sure Tator Tot is okay."

Sam cursed under his breath. For the second time that day, he had scared the poor kid. He peered over into the stall and nearly laughed out loud when he saw what Tyson was so concerned over. A miniature chestnut pony—so plump it looked more like a giant stuffed animal than a horse—was staring back at them beneath an abundant fringe of hair. The pony had somehow gotten his foot stuck in a narrow bucket. The scraping of the metal against the stone floor as it had tried to free himself had likely frightened Tator Tot into remaining frozen rather than lift its leg out.

Without thinking about it, Sam was in the stall, Tyson at his heels. He gently lifted the pony's hoof out of the bucket before carefully inspecting its leg for any cuts and bruises. "He looks okay," Sam reassured Tyson. "He must have pulled it down to get the rest of his grain out."

"Oh, Tots, you silly thing." Tyson brushed the long brown forelock out of the pony's eyes. Tator Tot nickered gratefully before giving the boy a nudge. "He thinks he can do everything the bigger horses can," Tyson said.

Crouching on his haunches beside the boy and his pony, Sam nodded. "There seems to be a lot of that going on around here." He gestured with his head toward Tator Tot. "Is he yours?"

Tyson wrapped his arms around the small pony's neck. "My daddy got him for me. He's my 'sponsibility."

A familiar feeling niggled within Sam. He'd once given a horse to someone he loved as a consolation prize. "Your daddy helps you out with him, though, right?"

The boy shook his head. "My daddy lives in Utah. He's training for the 'lympics. After he wins another gold medal, he's gonna come home, though," Tyson said proudly. "And then we're gonna be a real family."

"Tyson Campbell Johnson." Laurel's voice shot through the barn, followed by her hurried footsteps. "What have I told you about sneaking out of your grandparents' house at night?"

The boy snatched up the toy he'd absently discarded in the shavings. "I had to get Oreo's lovie. He can't sleep without it."

Sam slowly stretched to his full height and turned to see Laurel behind them. Her face was etched with panic, but her eyes were sparkling with that familiar agitation.

"Which explains why the dog is sound asleep on the bed and you're not." She crooked a finger at her son. "Grandma is beside herself with worry. You know she can't chase after you—especially when Grandpa isn't home. You're abusing your sleep-away privileges. If you can't behave at Grandma's, how can I let you spend the night at Cameron's this week-end?"

Tyson tucked his chin and slowly shuffled out of the

stall. "Night, Tator Tot," he murmured contritely.

Sam followed him out, securing the stall door behind them. The pony gave it a swift kick in solidarity with its master.

"March," Laurel commanded her son as she pointed toward the house. "Brush your teeth for a good solid minute and then I'll be up to tuck you in."

Head low, Tyson crept out of the barn.

The crisp night settled around them and Laurel's green eyes flickered with surprise when they landed on Sam, as though she'd just realized he was also in the barn. Her cheeks were flushed and her breasts were heaving enticingly beneath the teal puffy coat that hugged her body. The long legs that had been tantalizing his thoughts all day were clad in tight, brown jeans, ending in a pair of those furry Australian boots women liked so much.

She's taken, Sam reminded the parts of him that were firing up at the sexy way her teeth were chewing on her lip.

"Your son seems to really care for his pets," he said in an effort to fill the awkward silence that stretched between them.

Laurel grimaced as she wrapped her arms around herself. "He and his menagerie can be quite a handful."

And then we're going to be a real family, Tyson had said.

Sam had lost his 'real family'. And they weren't coming back. The insane jealousy he felt was squeezing painfully in his chest. He needed air and he needed to be away from this woman.

"I'm sure you'll be glad when his father gets back after the Olympics and can help you out." Sam wasn't sure why he said what he did or why he was even still standing there talking to her, but the look of shock and vulnerability that settled on her face was like a sucker punch to his gut.

"Is that what Tyson said?" She slumped against one of the pillars with a heavy sigh. "Dear Lord, he's going to be crushed next weekend when his father tells him he's getting married to someone else. I don't think even Mickey Mouse can make up for that."

As usual, Sam was having trouble following a woman's train of thought. "Tyson's father is marrying Mickey Mouse?"

She laughed, the lusty sound of it reverberating off the stone walls and settling in the vicinity of Sam's groin.

"I think Minnie Mouse might have some objection to that arrangement. Tyson's father is marrying a Victoria's Secret model. One of the angels with wings." She gestured wildly behind her back with her hands. "Nothing but the best for Straight Air Johnson."

Recognition dawned on Sam. Bryce Johnson was a big time snowboarder who was famous for his Air Crippler in the halfpipe—not to mention his wholesome smile that dominated the cereal aisle in the grocery store. Everybody loved the gold medal guy. But he was obviously a father who put his career before his child. And Sam immediately hated him for it.

Glancing over at Laurel, he caught a brief glimpse beneath the protective shield she wore. Sam recognized the traces of pain and abandonment that bracketed her mouth—facial expressions that most people probably mistook for haughtiness. And suddenly, without reason, Sam hated Bryce Johnson even more for whatever pain he might have caused the woman in front of him.

"He's an ass for hurting you both." Sam tried unsuccessfully to keep his words from sounding like a growl.

Laurel leapt away from the pillar. "You, too?" She paced a few steps. "Oh, my gosh, you just got here and even you think I'm pining after Bryce Johnson." She muttered something under her breath. "But then, why shouldn't you think what you want, everybody else does." She turned abruptly, her green eyes awash with indignation. "Let's get something straight, Captain Cowboy; Bryce and I are just friends. Sure, we were a little more than that once, obviously, but nothing serious. He was a youthful mistake on my part." She shrugged. "But one I don't regret for a single minute because then I wouldn't have Tyson."

Her voice broke slightly at the mention of her son's name, and the hint of her weakness did something to Sam's insides. *She's not taken*, his body was screaming.

"I'm happy for Bryce," she continued with an enthusiasm that sounded as though she were trying to convince herself of her words. "And Tyson will be, too. He's just got to get used to the idea, that's all. Not that it matters to you or anyone else in this town. But let the record state, I'm *not* waiting around for Bryce to come carry me off on his stupid snowboard."

Laurel shoved her hands into the pockets of her coat, daring him to contradict her. Sam was having trouble concentrating on her words. Instead, he was fixated on the pulse beating wildly along the white column of her neck. He wanted to put his lips there just to see how her body would react.

Clearly, he was going insane.

"What about you?" She gestured toward Tabitha with her stubborn chin. "You must have had it bad for your wife to want to keep her horse around; to skulk around a barn at night just to check on the darn thing."

It took him a minute to realize she was talking about Becky. Suddenly he was angry again. Angry at himself for totally forgetting why he'd come to the barn in the first place. And angry at the bewitching woman standing before him for making him forget Becky. *For making him crave a woman again.*

"Oh, GOD. I'M sorry." Laurel pressed her palms against her face. "That didn't come out the way I intended." What was it about this man that made her say such things? She lowered her fingers and forced herself to meet his stare. His expression was inscrutable, but she forged on just as she always did.

"I don't know what's wrong with me today. I'm really a nice person. Everyone thinks so. Believe it or not, I was voted Miss Congeniality of my high school class. You can ask anyone in town. Or have my mom show you the yearbook." Laurel's babbling tapered off, but Sam continued to level a hard stare at her. She swallowed painfully and tried again. "What I meant to say was your wife must have been a lovely person. Lucky, too, for you to go to so much trouble," she said softly before extending her hand to him. "Please, can we start over? If I'm going to be training her horse, I'd really like us to be friends."

His gaze drifted down toward her outstretched hand for a long heartbeat. Laurel gasped when he suddenly wrapped his fingers around hers and jerked her body flush against his chest. Her head fell back and she watched as his mouth softened just before his lips descended toward hers.

"Depends on what you mean by 'friends'," he drawled.

And then he was kissing her. It wasn't one of those tentative, nice-to-meet-you first kisses, either. Sam Gaskill kissed her with authority, as though he already possessed her, easily opening her mouth with his own and sliding his tongue home without so much as a 'may I please'. He tasted like hops and smelled like a man who spent all day outdoors. And Laurel, sexually starved woman that she was, submitted without protest, savoring the feel of his warm mouth melding with hers. Her hands slid beneath his leather jacket, trailing along the soft flannel shirt he wore to explore the contours of his chest. Sam's fingers fisted in her hair, anchoring her mouth beneath him. A soft moan escaped the back of her throat when her hips collided with his. He deepened the kiss with a groan of his own and the ache within Laurel's belly spread like wildfire.

"Please," she pleaded when he lifted his mouth to let his lips trail along her neck. Although, she couldn't for the life of her figure out what she was begging for. The man was a stranger, a client. Worse, he was an adrenaline junkie like Bryce. If Laurel was going to end her sexual drought, Captain Cowboy was the last guy she should choose.

Sam's hands found her ass and the last wisps of rational thought left Laurel's brain. His lips captured hers again, but now she was the one eagerly exploring. Her fingers bracketed the sides of his face as she delved deep into his mouth with reckless abandon. Desire, hot and fierce, coursed through her. It roared so loudly in her ears, she nearly missed the sound of Oreo's yipping.

Fortunately, Sam did hear it, quickly breaking away before her father's boots hit the barn floor. Laurel pulled in a few quick breaths while Sam put three giant paces between their bodies.

"I thought that was your truck out there, captain," her father called as he strode down the aisle, Oreo at his heels. "Is everything okay with the mare?"

Laurel sank down into the collar of her coat, hoping her

father wouldn't notice the beard burn Sam had left behind. The last thing she needed was her dad figuring out that she'd been climbing the man like a tree just moments before.

Sam turned back to face them, his face devoid of any telltale signs that he'd just had his tongue lodged halfway to her spleen. "No problem," he said. "I just wanted to check on her. Force of habit, I guess."

"Of course," her father said. "But she's safe and sound here, rest assured. That's not to say you're not welcome to stop by anytime. You should drop in earlier in the evenings when Laurel will be working with her. You'd be amazed at what my daughter can do when she gets her legs wrapped around a powerful animal. She's pure athleticism and poetry in motion."

The hot, hard gaze flickered briefly in Sam's eyes and she watched him swallow roughly. "I'm sure she is." Laurel felt the heat blazing on her cheeks before Sam shuttered his expression again. "But with the fire season approaching, I've got my hands full at the station." He looked at the palomino longingly, as though he was trying to glean some subliminal message from her, before turning back to her father. "I'll check in when I can. G'night." With nothing more than a nod, he was striding out of the barn. Laurel watched him go, unsure whether the emotion she was feeling was relief or disappointment.

CHAPTER FOUR

FIVE DAYS LATER, Laurel's thighs screamed in protest as she gingerly climbed the wide log steps leading to the forest service station. It turned out the mare wasn't the only one out of shape. Her evening sessions training Tabitha had reacquainted Laurel with muscles she hadn't used in years. The bulk of the riding she'd done during the past decade had been for pleasure—simple trail rides with guests and friends. But that kind of riding didn't prepare her for steering a horse through intricate patterns while using only her legs as a guide. Her father hadn't lied, though. Tabitha was well trained. It was a sad commentary on the state of her life that the horse would regain its suppleness and range of motion much more quickly than Laurel would.

The joy her mother was getting out of the whole experience helped to ease the ache in Laurel's cranky body, though. Freezing evening temperatures kept the ground hard, forcing them to work in the indoor arena, but her mother now had a reason to leave the house each day. And the bond her mom had already formed with the horse was uncanny. As much as Laurel hated the way her father had manipulated her into the whole situation, she had to admit his motives were good ones.

"Change in plans," Miranda said as Laurel stepped through the double doors and into the lobby of the sprawling log cabin that served as a base for the smokejumpers. "I can't have lunch. I have to shuttle a crew over to Glacier."

"Already? It flurried last night. How can Glacier be dry enough for a fire?"

Miranda rolled her eyes. "You've lived here all your life and you still think that's all we do. We have other jobs besides that. One of them is to get the parks ready for summer tourism season."

"In other words, we'll be picking up pine cones and un-clogging toilets for the next three days," Ace Clark said from where he sat on one of the four leather sofas in the station's vast two-story lobby area. The rest of the place seemed to be deserted, but he was carefully packing his gear into a giant backpack. Smokejumpers carried nearly a hundred pounds of equipment with them when they jumped into a fire zone— some of it in one of three packs strapped to their body and the rest stowed into pockets of their handmade Kevlar suits. Laurel had once tried to lift Liam's pack and she'd ended up on the ground with the heavy thing crushing her.

"Not exactly how I planned to spend my last few free nights before boot camp," Ace complained.

"Quit your grumbling," Miranda said. "You've been itching to jump out of an airplane for weeks now."

Ace's mouth turned up into a quick smile as he winked at Laurel. "The thrill of it is second only to sex."

"She wouldn't know," Miranda said with a laugh.

Laurel shot a murderous look at her cousin. "Hey!"

"I only meant that you're afraid of heights." Miranda responded innocently before she ticked off on her fingers. "And planes. And elevators. And caves."

Ace stood up, his brown eyes twinkling as he effortlessly hefted the backpack over his shoulder. "I'm happy to be your guide into any of the *thrills* you'd like to experience, Laurel. I promise you'll enjoy the ride. I haven't had any complaints yet."

Miranda made a gagging sound. Laurel shook her head with a smile. Ace Clark was tall, dark, and charming. And from what she'd overheard in the ladies room at The Drop Zone, he was telling the truth about women having no complaints. He just wasn't *that guy*. Laurel looked at most of the smokejumpers as the band of brothers she'd never had. She'd grown up with many of them and was related to a few more. The thought of ending her sexual drought with any one of them was ridiculous.

"Clark!" Sam Gaskill's voice boomed through the cavernous building, startling Laurel. "The drill commences at thirteen hundred."

With one exception.

Laurel glanced toward the back corner of the building to see Sam standing at his office door. Her breathing became less steady at the sight of him. He was wearing another pair of well-worn jeans, a long-sleeved, gray T-shirt with an army insignia emblazoned across his muscled chest and a hard look that had Ace muttering a "yes sir" before heading out past the reception desk and into the ready room.

"You're flying to Glacier?" Laurel whispered to her cousin. The entrance to Glacier National Park was only thirty miles from the station. She'd just assumed Miranda would be driving the crew in one of the two vans the forest service used to pick up the smokejumpers after they'd hiked out of a fire zone.

"Captain wants a practice run," Miranda replied. "I think he wants to assess if anyone in the crew might make a good spotter." The spotter's job was to identify a safe area for the smokejumpers to land. After Russ Edwards' accident, fingers had been pointed at the spotter's reliability to accurately gauge the wind and the conditions that accompanied a safe jump. He'd retired immediately, taking a job as a high school shop teacher.

Both women's eyes drifted to the loft above. Hanging from the railing was a red, white, and blue parachute with Edwards' name stitched along the bottom, along with the numeral one and an asterisk. The jagged rip in the chute had been sewn up, too. The makeshift memorial was a sobering reminder to all who entered the building that lives were on the line every time a crew went out.

"I should get going," Miranda said solemnly. Though she

hadn't been the pilot on the jump that cost Russ his life, Laurel knew her cousin still felt the loss of the captain as deeply as the rest of the smokejumpers.

Laurel quickly reached over and pulled her best friend in for a hug. "Be careful, okay."

Miranda scoffed. "I'm the best pilot they've got. I haven't dropped one of these idiots yet. And like Ace says, I haven't had any complaints either." She gave Laurel a saucy wave before following Ace toward the ready room.

Laurel stood in the now empty reception area, watching the dust motes dance in the midday sunlight that was streaming through the high windows. She told herself she should head to Starbucks and use her free lunch hour to cram in some studying for the CPA exam. But her eyes kept darting back to the open office door Sam had disappeared into.

She impatiently blew out a breath as her mind seemed to be fighting some internal war. Sam had obviously seen her. Even more exasperating, he'd overheard the conversation she'd had with Miranda and Ace. Laurel was embarrassed by their astonishing make-out session in the barn the other night, not to mention the way she'd given herself over to him without question. Each evening, she'd forced herself to remain in her apartment, listening—while her body practically vibrated with desire—as he came to the barn, presumably to check on Tabitha. Some nights he stayed for a few minutes, but the previous evening he'd hung out in the barn for an agonizing half hour.

Laurel wondered if he'd been waiting for her. Did he think she was that easy? That she'd fall into his arms a second time? Her face burned in humiliation because the message she'd given him that night was *yes, she was that easy*. Once again her impulsiveness had gotten the better of her.

She needed to clear things up with Sam if he was going to keep his horse at Whispering Breeze. Laurel needed to let him know that their close encounter of the lips was just an aberration. Because no matter how strong the sexual attraction, if she was going to bring someone into her life—into her son's life—it wouldn't be a man who risked his neck on a daily basis. Not this time.

Laurel hesitated outside Sam's office, watching as he performed the same task Ace had moments before—meticulously combing through the gear in his backpack. With his head bent and his jaw set, his long fingers rummaged through the contents as he appeared to be silently checking things off a list. She knew smokejumpers had to survive for forty-eight to seventy-two hours in the wilderness on each mission. The contents of a smokejumper's pack were essential to his or her survival when fighting a fire.

Her eyes drifted over her shoulder to Russ' solitary parachute. Sam was about to do what Russ had done—leap out of an airplane with nothing but the hope his jump cord wouldn't malfunction. Or that an errant wind wouldn't catch him and toss his defenseless body into the jagged limb of a tree.

A shiver of apprehension rocked through Laurel as she forced her gaze back into the office where it collided with Sam's own hard stare. He'd finished with his backpack. Now he waited silently with his hip propped against his desk and his arms crossed over his chest. This time Laurel's shiver was brought on by the hungry look in his eyes.

"Hi," she said feebly.

A terse nod and a quirk of an eyebrow were all she got in response.

"Umm, Miranda says you're going out on a jump?"

He nodded again. His arrogant silence was really beginning to get on Laurel's nerves.

"Well, were you even going to let someone know?" she demanded.

There was a painful pause before he finally spoke. "Someone being who exactly?"

Laurel huffed in annoyance. "Someone being Tabitha, perhaps?"

A corner of his mouth turned up at the idiocy of her words, and that made Laurel even more annoyed.

"What's she going to think when you don't show up tonight, hmm?"

A slow grin spread across his face, revealing a mesmerizing dimple on the right side of his mouth. The potency of his unexpected smile had Laurel reaching for the doorframe to keep her balance.

"I mean, you should let one of us know when you leave so if something should happen to Tabitha. . .well, we'd. . ." Her voice trailed off when he gently wrapped his fingers around her wrist and tugged her further into the office. Before she could react, the door was closed and her back was pressed against it while his mouth laid claim to hers.

He kissed her slowly this time, as though he was taking her as a prize for some victory. Laurel wanted to be offended, but the feel of his tongue sliding suggestively against hers had rendered any arguments mute. Her fingers had somehow found their way into his short, wavy hair, surprisingly soft between her fingertips. His hands slid underneath her cotton sweater where he let his palms skim over her skin, leaving a trail of arousing heat in their wake.

"Say what you really came here to say, Laurel," he murmured against her lips. "Admit that you wanted me to come upstairs and finish what we started the other night."

"Did not!" Laurel's protest might have sounded more convincing had her hands not been exploring Sam's ass.

He grinned again. This time it had a bit of a ruthless edge to it, making Laurel's insides somersault. Her body quickly made a liar out of her when Sam took possession of her lips one more time. She was sure he could feel the wild jolt within her as his mouth crushed hers. Her hips rolled restlessly at his, and she all but conceded defeat.

"It doesn't matter what I want." She practically wailed when his lips cruised to the spot near her ear that always made her knees buckle. "We can't do this."

"Mmm," he murmured against her skin. "I have to go on a jump in forty minutes. The rest is going to have to wait until I get back."

Laurel tapped her head against the back of the door in the hope of knocking some sense into her woozy brain. "No. That's why we can't do this. Now or ever."

His face was hard again as he pulled away and Laurel's body screamed at her in protest. She pressed her palms to the cool wood of the door to keep from digging her fingers into his T-shirt and pulling his body back against hers.

"*That's* what I came to tell you," she whispered.

"Do you ever say what you really mean?"

She hated that he had a point. "I have a little problem with impulsive behavior. But I'm working on it."

"And what, I'm too impulsive for you?" he drawled, angrily. "Or not impulsive enough?"

Laurel pointed to the jump pack sitting ominously in the corner of the room. "Too risky. Your job is too risky, which makes *you* too risky."

There was a brief flash of anguish in his eyes before he shuttered them behind the hard mask he'd likely perfected in the army. Laurel felt a spasm of guilt for having brought him any pain. But she had two hearts to protect—hers and Tyson's.

"Yeah," he said stoically. "It seems I'm destined to attract women who feel that way." He reached behind her and pulled open the door. "We should be back on Friday some-time. Tell Tabitha not to worry."

Laurel started for the reception area before turning back to Sam. "Be careful out there," she couldn't help saying.

His only acknowledgement was a stiff nod. Feeling a bit like a cold-hearted bitch, Laurel spun around and nearly careened into Jacqui Edwards, Russ Edwards' widow. She was headed toward Sam's office, Vin Kingston riding shotgun at her side.

Jacqui was the last person Laurel expected to see at the base. She'd been a fixture around the place for years, having worked the reception desk and as the file clerk. But just days after Russ had been laid to rest Jacqui took off without a word to anyone. Not that she and Laurel were particularly close. Still, Laurel liked the younger woman and her heart ached for her loss. Seeing the pain still so transparent in Jacqui's big brown eyes validated the decision she'd just made with Sam. Laurel couldn't expose her heart to the potential loss.

She gave the petite woman a warm smile. "Hey, Jacqui. I didn't know you were back." She gestured at Jacqui's dark hair, once long but now cut in a stylish pixie that framed her face and made her cheek bones look model worthy. "Great hair. That suits you."

"Thanks. I just got back, literally a few hours ago." Jacqui touched her hair, taking a slight step toward Vin.

Both Jacqui and Vin had been through the ringer these

past few months. Laurel was glad the young widow had someone helping her navigate the mourning process. Her thoughts flew to Sam. Who had helped him grieve? Surely he'd had more than a prize quarter horse to lean on?

"Vin," Sam said, interrupting her errant thoughts.

Laurel quickly reminded herself that she wasn't thinking of Sam that way. She couldn't.

She looked on as Vin introduced Jacqui to Sam, noting the proprietary way Vin stood beside Russ's widow. Despite the fact Vin was one of the very best men Laurel knew, she still hoped Jacqui had enough sense to protect her ravaged heart and not fall for a smokejumper twice.

"I wasn't expecting you to come in on your way from the airport," Sam said. "Unless… Were you just here to see…?" His gaze flicked to Russ's parachute and Laurel's heart squeezed.

"No. I thought we could talk about, um, my job," Jacqui replied.

Sam didn't bother to hide his relief. "That'd be great because things are a mess. I need to get someone in here pronto."

Ignoring Laurel, Sam ushered Jacqui into his office. Laurel tried not to let her disappointment show as she gave Vin a quick wave and made her way out of the station.

THE TWIN-ENGINE SHERPA flew a smooth circle over the

million acres of Glacier National Park. Sam had asked Miranda to stretch their flight out so he could assess the terrain. The day was clear and bright and, being new to the region, Sam wanted to commit as much of the park to memory as he could. Topography maps and the Internet were great tools, but if a fire or search and rescue came up, Sam needed to use his own mental images to be able to quickly formulate an initial assessment for headquarters without having to rely on others.

He glanced through the metal grate of his face mask across the aisle of the plane at the three smokejumpers on the bench facing him. Seven of the station's permanent team members were on board the plane, all looking relaxed in their helmets and jumpsuits despite the fact that each one knew this drill was an assessment of some kind. Since arriving in Montana, Sam had taken the initiative to spend time individually with each person on the year-round staff—whether it was on the base or in The Drop Zone. Or, in the case of Molly Rivers—one of the two female smokejumpers who worked for the forest service full-time—it was at the Laundromat on Sunday afternoon.

Sam liked what he saw in all the crew stationed at the base. They were a dedicated lot who trained every day to keep their bodies in peak physical shape. Based on his conversations with each one, he felt all of them were mentally tough enough to handle the grind of a long fire season. Even the guy sitting next to him.

Ace Clark stretched out his long legs, crossing his boots at the ankles. "Rumor has it Jacqui Edwards was in the station earlier," he said casually. The others on board looked up from their phones to listen in.

"She was. We can all breathe a sigh of relief because she's coming back to work," Sam announced. "I won't need to demote one of you to file clerk."

Molly, sitting on the other side of Ace, let out a relieved sigh. "Thank goodness."

"Yeah, we really missed her around the base," Garrett Broxson said from across the aisle.

"More like you missed the cowboy cookies she used to bring in," Jessica Mendez teased.

"Hey, don't tell my wife, but Jacqui makes a mean cookie," Broxson said with a grin.

"Six miles from the jump spot," Miranda radioed from the cockpit. The crew immediately sobered up, stowing their phones into the padded pocket sewn into their Kevlar jumpsuits before adjusting their helmets and sunglasses on their heads.

Sam watched as Doster Cohen searched the area with binoculars, looking for an adequate landing area. Practicing to be a spotter without having to worry about a raging fire overtaking the smokejumpers before they landed was a little like learning how to parallel park beside an empty curb. But Cohen had military experience at the job, and a conversation with his former CO revealed he was extremely efficient at the skill. That was enough for Sam to give him a shot. When Miranda began to descend and circle the Lake McDonald Valley, Cohen tossed several streamers out from the jump door. These would help him to determine the wind's speed and direction. Cohen watched the path of the streamers for a moment or two and then radioed instructions to Miranda in the cockpit.

The Sherpa banked right as it circled around the jump zone a second time, dropping to a cruising altitude of fifteen hundred feet. Cohen gave the cabin a thumbs up and Sam got to his feet. "Buddy up," he instructed the crew. "Clark, you're with me."

Somebody behind them muttered a good-natured "teacher's pet" at Clark as the group moved in a single-file line toward the jump door. Since they weren't worried about putting out a fire, Sam had selected a relatively easy landing area in the valley near Lake McDonald. They were splitting duty with the national park service, clearing some of the trails within Glacier. Sam's team had been given the area around the lake.

He glanced out the jump door to the green meadows dotted with yellow daffodils below. While recreational skydivers jumped from heights of over twelve thousand feet, smokejumpers typically jumped much shorter distances, allowing them to land into a more compact target zone. There was a world of difference between a serene sixty-second free-fall to earth and the ten-second hurtle to the ground smokejumpers experienced.

Sam checked to make sure his static line was secured to the aircraft. For smokejumpers, the static line functioned essentially as a ripcord; once he exited the plane, Sam would have a few seconds of slack before the static line pulled the parachute from its pack. In the unlikely event the parachute didn't deploy, Sam would have another second to manually operate his reserve parachute. He mouthed the same silent refrain he uttered before every jump, praying he wouldn't break his ass or anything else when he kissed the ground.

Cohen tapped him on the shoulder and Sam reflexively stepped out of the plane. Two seconds later, his parachute inflated behind him with a jerk. The sheet got air but not enough to slow his descent that much. He pulled his feet and knees together, careful to keep his legs slightly bent as the ground rose up to meet him. Smokejumpers were trained to hit the ground by tucking their body into a ball and rolling—technically referred to as a parachute landing fall. When perfectly executed, they first touched the ground with the balls of their feet, tucking and rolling in the direction of the landing while absorbing the gravity of the fall with their calves, thighs, hips, and the sides of their back. The elapsed time for the full maneuver was barely a second.

The move was second nature to Sam and he completed it without injury. He quickly shucked his parachute over his shoulder so he could watch and assess the rest of his team's landings. He should have known Clark would execute the move with more grace than a cat. But he made a mental note Broxson needed to shed a few pounds to make his landing look effortless. Rivers rolled onto the extra padding sewn into her jumpsuit and Ace yelled something about marshmallows across the meadow at her. The rest of the crew landed without incident, all of them sporting endorphin-fueled smiles on their faces.

"Glacier Creek transport to base," Sam heard Miranda's voice on the radio he carried. "Papa and the Bad News Bears have landed. Commence the com transfer."

There was a chuckle at the other end of the radio when Tyler Dodson's voice came over it. "I take it everyone is still in one piece, captain?"

"We landed on an effing cushioned mattress, for crying out loud," Clark grumbled from beside Sam. "The degree of difficulty was negative ten. Everybody had better be in one piece or they're facing boot camp with the rookies next week."

Sam's opinion of Clark rose even higher. Clearly, the guy was into the job.

"Everyone is intact and accounted for," Sam said into the radio. He watched as the crew was already shedding their Kevlar jumpsuits, pulling items out of the pockets and shoving them into their packs. They then worked in teams of two to secure their parachutes, carefully checking them for any damage before folding and stowing them back into their jump packs.

"Well, you little scouters enjoy your s'mores on the lake," Dodson was saying. "Ferguson, Kingston, and I will just work our asses off getting this paperwork ready for the start of boot camp next week."

"Try not to staple your hand to the desk," Ace called as he rolled up his parachute.

"Check in if you need more marshmallows." Dodson joked. "Glacier-one out."

Sam tucked the radio inside the pocket of the down shell he'd brought with him. Normally, smokejumpers wore standard-issue fire gear beneath their Kevlar, but since they'd be wielding axes and kombi shovels to clear trails, they'd all donned comfortable clothing they could work and sleep in. He shoved his helmet into his backpack and grabbed his jump pack.

Broxson and two of the others were busy unpacking the box of equipment Cohen had dropped after they'd all landed. He passed out the four chainsaws to one member of each of the teams of two. Then he strapped the extra water to his own pack while Clark took the other. The afternoon sun was warm on their backs as they hiked two miles east toward the Lake McDonald Ranger Station. Along the way, they made quick work of trees and shrubs overtaking the trail.

Nestled among hundred-foot red cedar trees—some as old as five hundred years—the ranger station looked out over Lake McDonald, a long, narrow nine and half mile body of water that was the largest of the seven hundred and sixty lakes in the park. The vast, blue waters rippled in the spring breeze. Sam stood for a moment admiring the majestic view from the covered front porch of the cabin. Growing up military, he'd lived all over the world, but he didn't think he'd ever seen anything more beautiful than the view he was enjoying now.

The station wasn't staffed during the winter months, and the crew's first task was to make sure it was habitable for the forest ranger arriving for the summer. Sam punched in the code to the log cabin's front door before throwing it wide open. The movement was met with a wild fluttering when a family of bats dive-bombed Sam's head before they made their way out of the cabin. Clark doubled over in laughter as Molly Rivers patted Sam on the shoulder.

"Consider yourself initiated, captain," she said as the rest of the team joined Clark in laughter.

Sam turned to find Broxson with his cell phone out recording the moment. "Hey, remember when Kiffin nearly wet his pants at the bat family. You get points for not squealing like a girl, captain."

They laughed again and Sam relaxed at the sound of it. He'd planned this outing to test some of his crew. Apparently they were testing him, too. Of course, the odds he'd ever squeal like a girl were pretty much nil, but he liked the idea they were coming to accept him as part of the team.

"Bats are practically the state bird of Texas, Broxson." Sam stepped into the cabin, careful not to disturb any more

winter guests. If bats could get in, so could a rattler. He
pulled his pulaski from his pack, just in case. Molly flipped
on the generator, bringing the station to life. The three-room
building was dusty with a sprinkling of sparkly bat shit, but
with a half hour of effort it would be habitable for the crew
tonight.

Clark was already dumping his gear and stripping down
to his Henley and jeans. "I'm allergic to dust, captain," he
said as he tossed a plunger at Broxson. Then he grabbed his
own pulaski, a kombi shovel, and one of the chainsaws.
"We've got several hours of daylight left. How about if
Broxson, Kiffin, and I head out to the campground over at
Howie Ridge and knock out whatever work needs to be done
there. You girls can get this place shipshape and still have
time to catch a couple of trout for dinner."

"Oh, no you don't," Mendez said. With fingers decorat-
ed in fire engine red nail polish, she grabbed one of the
chainsaws. "Just because I'm female, doesn't mean I'll do
your cooking and cleaning, Ace Clark." She gestured at
Ryder and Simms. "Come on you two, let's head over to the
falls and clear out that trail."

Simms winked at Clark as he pulled a fishing pole and a
tackle box out of the kitchen pantry. "That's the best spot in
this area for trout anyway. Never let it be said Jessica can't
bring home the dinner and fry it up in a pan," he said.
Mendez stomped off, Simms and Ryder in tow, while the
rest of the crew laughed. With a quick salute, Clark and his

team took off in the opposite direction.

"Don't make me have to come out there and rescue your sorry asses," Molly called after them. She shrugged when she met Sam's gaze. "Ace has ants in his pants," she said. "Never could sit still." She glanced around the cabin. "I've got this if you want to explore the area. There's a lookout tower a few miles toward the trail head. The path to it could likely stand some weeding. The view from the top will give you some perspective on the trails we'll be working on the next few days." She grabbed a broom out of the pantry where Ace had found the plunger.

Sam wasn't sure exactly when he'd lost control of his team, but with boot camp and a long fire season stretching ahead of them, they all needed to blow off a little steam. Yanking the reins back now would only stoke the resentment that had begun to fizzle out. He grabbed his pulaski and a kombi shovel and headed out, following the signs to the trailhead located near the shore of the lake.

"Keep an eye out for bears," Molly called out just before he made his way off the circular driveway. Sam felt his own endorphins and adrenalin kick in. A confrontation with a bear would definitely suit him today. It wouldn't be any worse than the showdown he'd had with Laurel Keenan earlier.

He tromped through the brush that threatened to over-take the trail, chopping at it with his pulaski as he walked. *The woman was infuriating.* One minute, she was kissing him like she wanted to crawl inside of him and the next she was shoving him away, telling him he was too "dangerous", too "risky". She was the dangerous one. Dangerous to his mind and body. Every freaking time she came within ten feet of him he wanted to grab her up, hoist her over his shoulder, and haul her off to someplace private where he could unleash the impulsive, passionate woman Laurel was clearly trying to keep contained.

Sam dug out the root of a vine and yanked at it with his hand before tossing it through some trees. He was damned tired of women telling him he was too much of a risk; as if putting himself on the line for his country was something to be ashamed of. He didn't need that in his life.

He swiped at the sweat forming on his brow, taking a moment to glance out over the lake. Pulling in a deep breath, Sam refocused his mind on the work he and the team needed to get accomplished over the next seventy-two hours. He'd committed his crew to clear sixty miles of trails on the south side of Going to the Sun Road, the fifty-mile road that bisected the park. There were several campgrounds that needed to be checked along the way. Three days of hiking, camping, and physical labor should be enough to keep his mind off Laurel Keenan and her mind-blowing kisses.

You haven't changed. He heard Becky's disappointed words in his head. *You'd still rather run into a fire than face your feelings,* she'd accused. She'd been right that horrifying day she'd taken off on Tabitha in a rage, hating him. But he'd rather hurl his body out of a perfectly good airplane than sit around and pick apart his relationship or discuss his fucking feelings. He slashed at the brush until his shoulders ached. And he wasn't going to change. No way was he giving up the adrenalin rush his work gave him. Not even for a woman who kissed liked Laurel Keenan.

CHAPTER FIVE

"**A**RE YOU SURE you have everything?" Laurel asked for what felt like the hundredth time.

Her mother sighed as she wheeled herself toward the SUV her dad was busy loading their suitcases into. "Sweetheart, relax. Whatever Tyson forgets, Bryce will be able to get in California. And Dad and I are only staying in Spokane two nights, but if we need something, they have some wonderful shopping."

"Which means I'll be spending all weekend in moldy antique shops and fabric stores," her father said, trying to look annoyed when Laurel knew the truth was he doted on his wife. "Of course, if we don't get Tyson in the car, we'll miss meeting up with Bryce in the Spokane airport this afternoon."

Laurel walked inside the barn where her son was holding court with Oreo, Truman, Cheech and Chong—the alpacas her father used as pack animals on trail rides—and Pirate, the one-eyed barn cat. "You all had better be on your best behavior while I'm away," he was saying, practically repeating the speech Laurel had given to her son moments before.

"Listen to Mommy and don't wander off. I'll see you again in five wake-ups." She gnawed on her lip as she watched him, one-by-one, hug each animal before racing into Tator Tot's stall to wrap his arms around the pony's neck.

"Mickey Mouse is waiting," she called to him.

Oreo darted between their feet as they walked hand in hand toward the SUV.

"I wish you were coming, too," Tyson said.

Laurel fought against the tightness in her throat. "We've been over this, Tyson. This is your special trip with Daddy. Besides, I have to study, remember?"

"You're already smart, Mommy," Tyson argued.

Laurel smiled in spite of her disappointment that Bryce would be getting this experience with their son. "What does Miss Ivy always say?"

"The richest people learn something new every day," they both said together.

Unable to stop herself, she picked him up. Normally he'd protest that he was too big to be treated like a baby, but today Tyson wrapped his arms around her neck and stared solemnly at her. "Me and Daddy are gonna miss you," he said before hugging her tightly.

Her parents exchanged worried looks. It was hard to tell how Tyson was going to react to Bryce's announcement. Laurel only hoped the boy's father had read some of the parenting books she'd been sending him.

"Who's ready to go to Disneyland?" her father called out

with a clap of his hands.

Tyson jumped down from her embrace and, with one more squeeze of Oreo, he scrambled into his booster seat. Her father helped her mom into the passenger seat.

While her dad stowed the wheelchair in the back, Laurel's mom quietly tried to reassure her. "Everything will be fine." Laurel had lost count of the number of times her mother had uttered those words over the years, whether she was saying them to herself or her daughter.

Despite her misgivings, Laurel nodded and gave her mother a hug. "Enjoy your weekend," she said as she closed the door.

"We'll call you when we hand him off to Bryce," her father said with a wave.

Oreo plopped down on Laurel's boot, whimpering as the SUV pulled away. They stood there long after her family disappeared down the driveway, until Truman gave her a soft butt with his head reminding Laurel that she had things to do. Knowing she'd be a bit of a basket case, she'd taken the day off work under the guise of getting some studying done. But the idea of ten chapters detailing income taxation made her eyes cross, so she headed into the barn instead.

The morning was warm and sunny. Laurel decided to take advantage of the weather by giving Tabitha a workout. With Oreo and Truman looking on, she put the mare in the cross-ties and cleaned the horse's feet with a hoof pick. Tabitha shifted her body into the brush when Laurel curried her off.

"You like that, eh," she said as she gave the horse a gentle pat on the rump. "Well, at least one of us won't be lonely that much longer. Your daddy comes home tonight."

Tabitha stomped a foot as Laurel pulled the latigo strap on the saddle and cinched it tight on the mare's girth. She brushed her fingers down the horse's neck to sooth her while threading the strap through a D-ring on the saddle and tying off the latigo neatly, the process similar to tying a necktie.

"Did you miss him?" she asked while she gently placed the bit between the horse's teeth. "Don't tell anyone, but I missed him," she admitted to the animals assembled in the barn. "I know, I know, nothing can happen between us. But you have to admit, he's pretty hot." Laurel pulled the bridle over Tabitha's head. "And a really great kisser."

Laurel guided the mare over to the mounting block and climbed into the saddle. Oreo and Truman trotted beside them as they made their way out into the bright sunshine. "A girl can only imagine what other things that guy of yours does well," she said wistfully.

Unfortunately, Laurel's body wasn't having any trouble imagining what Sam Gaskill could potentially do with that talented mouth of his. Or his very capable fingers. Tabitha took off at a fast trot before Laurel even realized she'd been squeezing her thighs together. She relaxed her legs and slowed the horse back down to a walk.

"Anything that happens with Sam would be impulsive,"

she admonished herself. "And I'm not impulsive anymore." Tabitha looked over her shoulder at Laurel. The horse's big, brown eyes were full of disbelief. "Well, I'm trying not to be." The mare snorted and swished her tail.

"Yeah, thanks for the support." Laurel spurred the mare on, shoving images of Sam out of her mind as she lost herself in an effort to become one with the animal beneath her.

TEN HOURS LATER, Laurel was jerked awake by the ringing of her cell phone. Peeling a page of her textbook from where it had stuck to her cheek, she sat up groggily. Night had fallen and a steady rain was pelting the roof. Oblivious, Oreo was curled into a ball at the other end of the sofa, snoring softly. Laurel checked the caller ID.

"Ivy," she said into the phone. "What's up?"

It was nine-thirty on Friday night, and Laurel really hoped her friend hadn't downed too many appletini's while stalking Liam at The Drop Zone. Miranda was working tonight, which meant Laurel would be the one to have to rescue their friend. She glanced down at the camisole top and comfy Hello Kitty sleep pants she'd pulled on when she'd finished with Tabitha that morning. No wonder she'd fallen asleep. Ivy was going to really owe her one if she had to get dressed *and* go out in the rain.

"Hey, you." Thankfully, Ivy sounded relatively sober. "I've decided that my new favorite Hugh Grant movie is

Notting Hill. Although, I'm watching *Music and Lyrics* now and who's to say what will happen."

Laurel stood up and stretched, relieved that Ivy was safe and sound at home, apparently enjoying a Hugh Grant marathon. She looked down at the creased page in her textbook, wishing she could enjoy a little of the Brit's smile right about now. Instead, she wandered into the kitchen and put a pod of coffee in the Keurig. Given how little studying she'd gotten done today, she needed some caffeine to meet her goals.

"What's your favorite Hugh film?" Ivy asked.

"*Sense and Sensibility*," Laurel answered without hesitation. "*Love Actually* would be a close second."

"Oh, I love when he does the little dance in that one. I wish our elected officials were as much fun as his character. Almost as much as I love him wrapped in a towel in *Two Weeks' Notice*." Ivy paused. "Wait, I think that one's my favorite Hugh Grant movie."

The coffee finished brewing. Laurel pulled out her mug, poured in some cream and took a sip. Ivy had a tendency to wax on when she was in the midst of one of her movie marathons.

"Listen, Ivy, I've still got"—Laurel frowned as she leafed through her textbook—"six more sections of business law to get through tonight. I want to knock out as much studying as I can while Tyson is away. Can I take a rain check on Hugh Grant?"

"Oh sure." Ivy said. "I just wanted to check in and see how you were doing out there. Alone. In the rain."

She'd been doing just great until Ivy reminded her of her situation.

"I'm fine." She glanced over at Oreo, who was sound asleep. Not that he'd be any help if something came up. "The barn is closed up tight," she lied. She just realized she'd slept through night check. As soon as she hung up with Ivy, she'd go secure the barn.

"Well, Hugh and I will be here all night. Call me if you need a study break."

"I'll do that," Laurel said as she slid her feet into her Ugg boots. "Let's plan on dinner tomorrow night. Unless, of course, you're too busy with Hugh."

"I was planning on spending tomorrow night with Channing Tatum, but a girl's gotta eat. Call me in the morning."

Laurel disconnected with Ivy but kept her phone in her hand as she made her way into the barn. Thunder boomed outside the wide-open doors and she hurried to pull them closed. A scream caught in her throat when a bolt of lightning lit up the barn, exposing Sam Gaskill lurking in the dark.

He was the picture of natural vitality sitting on the tack box outside of Tator Tot's stall, dressed in dark jeans, and an untucked white button-down shirt. The sleeves were rolled up to reveal his tightly corded, tan forearms. The sight of him unnerved her. Not just because he was unexpected, but because of the gnawing want the man always seemed to stir up in her.

"What are you doing here?" *Stupid question.*

Her eyes had adjusted to the dim light in the barn. She watched as Sam lifted a bottle of beer to his lips and took a long pull. Even the way the muscles in his neck contracted as he swallowed was sexy.

"I'm checking on my horse," he said, finally.

"You mean your *wife's* horse."

His head snapped around and his amber eyes bored into hers. Laurel shifted uneasily. She'd gone too far again. She had no idea why she continued to play this game with him.

"My *late* wife's horse."

Lightning crackled in the distance as if to punctuate his words.

Laurel wrapped her arms around her middle, wishing she'd pulled on a jacket or something to cover up her revealing cami. "Either way, the company's likely better at The Drop Zone tonight."

"Company's just fine right here," he drawled before turning his head back toward Tabitha's stall and taking another drink from his beer.

A rumble of thunder shook the barn and the horses groaned in their stalls, their hooves moving restlessly over the shavings. Laurel could honestly say she knew how they felt. She turned her back on Sam and began shuffling down the aisleway, checking water buckets and stall doors as she went. When she turned back, he was still there, eyes closed and the beer bottle dangling from his long fingers. She wanted him to leave. Unfortunately, not quite as much as she wanted him to stay. And that was the problem.

The words were out before she could stop them. "The storm is going to take a while to move off. I have coffee upstairs."

He was still for an agonizingly long moment before he turned to face her again. His mouth was drawn tight. "You don't want to invite me upstairs, Laurel. You're working on your impulsiveness issues, remember?"

"Yeah, but right now, you're looking a whole lot more interesting than my business law study guide." And just like that, Impulsive Laurel was back in charge.

WHAT THE HELL was he doing here? After three days clearing trails and sleeping outside, Sam was tired and sore. He should have stayed in the A-frame, downed his beer, and hit the sack. But he couldn't seem to get this woman off his mind. Laurel had told him very plainly that she didn't want him. The trouble was her body sang a very different tune every time he got near her. And Sam couldn't quite get his own body to settle down and stop humming that song.

Being the jerk that he was, he knew the good girl persona Laurel was so desperately trying to hide behind wouldn't take much work to peel away. Hell, deep down, she was as impulsive as Sam was. Sam had gambled she wouldn't turn him away, and it had just paid off.

She'd made it clear he wasn't what she was looking for long-term and that was fine with Sam. He wasn't looking for happily ever after either. That ship had sailed. But he was looking for happy tonight. Whether she knew it or not, so was she. As he followed Laurel's Hello Kitty-clad ass up the stairs to the loft, he vowed he'd make sure she wouldn't regret her decision in the morning.

Sam wasn't sure what he expected Laurel's home to look like, but the elegant apartment with bleached wood floors and sloped cherrywood ceilings looked more like something out of *Architectural Digest* than a hayloft above a barn. Three large dormer windows spread along the length, and French doors at one end kept the space from feeling closed in. Pendant lamps mixed with canned lights gave the place a welcoming glow even on the stormy night.

At the loft's entrance there was a white galley kitchen with a center island constructed from an antique wood cabinet. The other end of the island was held up by giant milk pails that were painted a vivid blue. A quick glance to his left revealed a sliding door constructed of weathered wood. The door partially concealed a bedroom large enough for a queen-sized iron bed and two craftsman dressers. Lightning flashed in the window high above the bed, momentarily giving the room a mystical glow.

Sam's boots were loud on the floor as he walked over to a table in the center of the loft. It was stacked with open books and a laptop. Obviously she'd been too absorbed in her studies to hear his truck on the gravel a half hour ago.

Oreo yipped from his perch on the leather sofa next to the table. The dog nearly toppled off when he stood on the cushioned arm to bark at Sam. As he had the other day, Sam grabbed the dog by the scruff of its neck and stared into Oreo's eyes. No commands were necessary this time. The dog swallowed a gulp before subduing. Sam gently laid him on a round dog bed in a corner by another sliding door—this one painted red like a barn.

He gestured at the door, assuming her son was asleep behind it. "Tyson?"

Laurel leaned her hips against the island in the kitchen and shook her head. "With his dad."

Her mouth took on a wistful expression and Sam wondered whether she missed the boy. *Or the boy's father.* Something stirred inside of him—lust, most likely—and he prowled over to the kitchen. It didn't matter who she was missing. Laurel was his tonight. He had every intention of making her forget whatever was making her sad.

Sam carefully put the empty beer bottle on the island before placing his hands on the wood, one on either side of her. Laurel sucked in a sharp breath when his hips came within an inch of hers.

"Can I, um, can I get you something else to drink? Coffee maybe?"

He closed the gap between their bodies and her pulse began its telltale wild beat at her neck. "I didn't come up here for coffee, Laurel." Sam sealed his mouth over the soft flesh at her throat. She tasted like lemon and smelled like summer, and when she sighed at the contact, the zipper on his jeans became damn near unbearable. "Last chance, Laurel," he said against her skin. "I need you to be sure you want me here tonight. *All night.*"

"You'd really leave now?" She sounded so incredulous, he had to pull back to look at her face. A sexy pink flush had formed on her skin and her nipples were hard beneath her flimsy top.

Not without a team of horses dragging me out, he wanted to shout. "If that's what you really want," the soldier deep inside of him said instead.

She gnawed on her lip as she fiddled with the buttons on his shirt. The rain pelted the roof even harder, the beat of it synchronizing with the blood pounding in Sam's groin.

"It's just sex, right?" she whispered, as though she were trying to convince herself. "We're both grownups. No one needs to know."

That last part stuck in his craw a bit. Not that he went around boasting of his sexual conquests, but it sounded like she was ashamed of who or what he was. Damn it, why did women always have to make sex so complicated?

He hadn't realized she'd undone the buttons until she'd

spread the sides of his shirt wide and her lips were blazing a path over his pectoral muscles. He felt her smile against his skin when his cock jumped at the contact. "You can stay all night," she murmured. "And if you're really a good boy, Captain Cowboy, I might even throw in breakfast."

That was pretty much all the encouragement he needed. Sam let her have her fun, tangling her fingers in his chest hair a moment longer, but when her hands headed south toward his zipper, he cupped her ass and lifted her onto the island so they were face-to-face. Laurel was breathing deeply, but she met his stare without blinking, her green eyes challenging. She would likely be as impulsive at sex as she was with the rest of her life, and the thought suddenly made Sam hard as hell.

She draped her arms around his neck, cocking her head so her ponytail swished from side to side. "Are we gonna do this or not, captain?"

"Oh, we're gonna do this." He leaned in and nipped at the corner of her mouth. "Multiple times, in fact." Sam swallowed her gasp when his lips crushed hers.

He let himself get lost in the sweet taste of her mouth and the intoxicating feel of her body rubbing against his. Desperate for more of her, he slid his fingers beneath the thin fabric of her top. A soft, keening sound escaped the back of Laurel's throat when he found her pebbled nipples. She wrapped her thighs around his waist and arched her body toward his in invitation. Breaking their kiss, Sam let his lips trail over her feverish skin as he nudged the spaghetti straps of her top down to her elbows.

Laurel nearly jumped off the counter when Sam gently blew on her aroused nipple. "Sam, please." She embarrassed herself by begging.

She felt his chest rumble with a laugh. Laurel was about to end the drought of a lifetime and the damn man thought it was funny. She squeezed her legs around him more tightly. He got the message and flicked his tongue over her before taking the nipple in his mouth and sucking. Laurel nearly exploded right then and there. Tears stung her eyes she was so frenzied—both to find the release she hadn't had from a real man in years and to make this last more than three minutes.

"Please what, Laurel," he teased.

"I-I…It's been, um, kind of a while," she admitted. "I'm not sure how long my body can hold out before we get to the good stuff."

His chest rumbled again. "Are you saying this isn't good?"

Sam teased her other nipple with his tongue and she thought she might shatter right there. "This is good," she said with a gasp. "Really good. That's the problem."

He slowly lifted his head and his gaze landed on her chin, then her cheeks. It lingered on her mouth before finally meeting her eyes. What she saw reflected there stunned her. *He knew.*

He understood. Her body sagged with relief, and if she hadn't been wrapped around him like a sloth, she might have fallen to the floor in a puddle.

He placed a gentle kiss on her lips. "You've got some catching up to do. Nothing to be ashamed of. But the 'good stuff' might be more enjoyable if we take this someplace else. Someplace where I can touch all of you." Laurel shivered at his words. "And where you can return the favor."

She kissed him frantically as he carried her into her bedroom, mostly because she had to but also because she wanted to distract him so he wouldn't notice her messy room. Of course, it didn't work. He tossed her down on her unmade bed before quickly giving her bedroom the once over with that military way of his.

"I wasn't expecting company," she explained, perhaps a tad too defensively.

"Mmm," was all he said when he sat down on the edge of the bed and began pulling off his boots. His shirt was next. Then Sam stood and undid the button on his jeans.

Panic began to set in. Technically, it had been longer than "a while" since she'd actually done this, and Laurel wondered if she'd be able to keep up. She would die if she did something wrong or, worse, somehow disappointed Sam.

"You're taking off your clothes?" Oh damn, she'd said that out loud.

To his credit, Sam didn't flinch. Or laugh. Instead, he continued to methodically strip in front of her, pushing his jeans and his briefs—*red Calvin's, Laurel noticed with a sigh*—down his muscled thighs.

"I've found that the good stuff is a lot more fun if you're naked," he said as he bent to pull his jeans over his feet. When he stood back up, Laurel sucked in a breath; his aroused body was so beautiful. He must have heard her because that hot, hard gaze of his landed on her mouth. She licked her lips, the reflexive gesture eliciting an immediate response from the part of him she most wanted to touch right now.

He strode purposefully toward the night stand and laid several foil-wrapped condoms between a glass of water and the assortment of creams Ivy kept foisting at Laurel.

"Of course, if you'd like me to do the honors," he said as he climbed on the bed. "I certainly can."

Laurel sat up quickly. The idea of him peeling off her clothes was both arousing and terrifying. She needed to keep some control of the situation and his hands on her too soon might not be a good idea. Not if she wanted this to last longer than the storm outside. Reaching down, she pulled her cami up from her midriff and over her head. It was Sam's turn to haul in a breath. His appreciative nod spurred her on and she kicked off her sleep pants. She was immensely glad she'd worn lace bikini panties today and not the Wonder Woman undies Tyson had insisted she buy to match his.

"Leave them," Sam growled when she tucked her fingers inside the elastic to pull them off.

Lightning flashed seconds before the thunder shook the barn. Sam didn't seem to notice as he crawled toward her. She shivered despite the warm heat radiating off his bare skin. And then he did something that caught her completely by surprise—he reached up and gently pulled the elastic band from her hair.

"It's a mess," she whispered when he brushed her hair out with his fingers.

"Why must women always complain about their hair?" he murmured. "FYI, it's not the first thing a guy notices."

Laurel's laugh sounded more like a snort. "Not surprised." She wanted to ask him what he'd first noticed about her but his lips had found the erogenous spot where her neck met her shoulder and she was too busy melting into the bed. Sam's body covered hers and her hands, tentatively at first, slid along the muscled planes of his back.

"This," he said when his lips began to nibble at the corners of her mouth.

"This, what?" Laurel was falling into a very nice sensual haze and she was having trouble keeping up with his words.

"This is what I first noticed about you. Your stubborn, outrageous, sexy-as-hell mouth."

Before Laurel could respond, he'd opened her lips with his and his tongue was ruthlessly dueling with hers. She hated how vulnerable and exposed she was with this man. How he seemed to know what she was thinking. But right now, she loved the things his mouth and his hands were doing to her body to object too much.

His fingers reached beneath her panties to trace her wet seam. She sighed in pleasure and before she knew it, her panties were down around her knees, Sam's lips kissing a path down her thighs. *Right there,* she wanted to scream as she arched her hips toward him. Ignoring her, he yanked the scrap of lace over her feet and tossed them to the floor before crawling up her body and delving into her mouth again.

Her hands skimmed the dimples on his ass, forcing a moan from deep in the back of Sam's throat. His reaction empowered Laurel and she trailed her hands up his sides before pushing at his chest in an effort to reverse their positions. Despite the fact he could easily subdue her, Sam let Laurel have her way. He gripped her waist and rolled onto his back, taking her with him. His jaw clenched tightly at the contact with his arousal when she straddled him.

Sam's hands went immediately to her breasts, cupping them in his palms.

"I might have noticed these second," he said. "But only because it was a chilly morning."

She swatted at his wrists. "Figures. But now it's my turn to explore."

He looked like he might object, but then his hands settled at her hips where his fingers gently traced circles on the tender skin there.

"Do your best." His amber eyes were amused despite the challenge.

She sensed the well-contained power beneath the surface of his body and she knew he would only let her have the reins for so long. It had been an eternity since she'd had a sexy man beneath her thighs and she intended to take full advantage of the situation.

Leaning over him, Laurel breathed in his musky smell when her lips traced the rounded muscle on his shoulder. Her hair trailed along his skin as her mouth made its way toward his sternum and lower toward their target of the dark nipples on his chest. She scraped her teeth over the first one, already tight with desire, and his cock nudged enticingly against her inner thigh. Desire, fierce and hot, shot to her core and her hands shook slightly when she took him in her fingers.

Sam's eyes slammed shut and he let out a hiss of pleasure as she stroked the velvet skin repeatedly between her palms. The pressure from his fingertips against her skin increased and she rocked her hips over him. His fingers were sliding between her entrance in an instant and she moaned at the pleasure of it, all the while gripping him more tightly. He swore violently when her breathing fractured and her body began to tremble.

"Come here," he commanded, pulling her hands away from his hard length before grabbing her hips and guiding her forward so that she was seated just above his mouth.

"Oh." Laurel moaned when his tongue delved into the spot where his fingers had just been. She wrapped her hands around the cool metal headboard to keep her knees from buckling from the sheer pleasure that was coursing through her body. Thunder roared overhead while Sam's relentless mouth banked up an internal storm within Laurel. Her climax overtook her gradually, like a slow rain after a lengthy drought, until she finally came in a powerful wave of heat, a thousand pinpoints of lights descending behind her eyelids. She threw back her head in relief, calling out Sam's name like a hallelujah chorus.

His lips were kissing the inside of her thighs and his fingers were kneading her butt when Laurel came back to earth. She rocked back onto her heels and tossed her hair over her shoulder.

"Thank you," she murmured against Sam's mouth, her hands reaching for his erection. "Thank you very, very much."

He laughed, the rich sound of it melting Laurel a little bit more, before he quickly sobered again. "No," he said when her hand wrapped around him. His heart was hammering beneath the other palm Laurel had flat on his chest. "No more playing. Now we get to the good stuff."

"That last part was pretty damn good."

"This part will be better than damn good," he said just before executing a move that had her breathless beneath him.

"You must be very fluid with a parachute." She traced a finger over his chest, trying not to let the sensual fog lift so she'd be thinking about Sam jumping out of airplanes—into fires.

His eyes locked with hers. "Put the condom on me," he demanded. "That's all I want you thinking about right now."

She did what he asked, still in awe of the way he could read her mind. But then he was slowly pushing into her tight body and she lost all coherent thought except for the intimate feel of him inside of her. Lowering her lashes so he wouldn't gain any more access to her emotions, she drew him in deeper, letting the heat unfurl in her belly again.

"That's a girl," he murmured next to her ear. "You feel so damn good."

He began to move, slowly, almost reverently at first. But Laurel's insides were on fire again and her hips refused to stay still beneath his hot, heavy weight. She nipped at his shoulder. Message received, he picked up the pace as Laurel strained to meet his every move. Wrapping her legs behind his back to give him better access to her core, she cried out when he thrust against her. Her fingernails dug into the muscles of his back, slick from their exertion, as her head thrashed from side to side. Sam kept up the pace, all the while whispering lusty words of encouragement in her ear. This time, her climax came in a powerful wave, blinding her with its intensity. Sam stilled above her, poised on outstretched arms that shook slightly as he watched her shatter. Time stopped for a moment. Then his mouth found hers and she melted into him. Laurel rocked her hips and squeezed him tightly until he came in a rush, her name tumbling from his lips in a low growl.

CHAPTER SIX

S AM WOKE WITH a start as something cold and wet nudged his chin. He caught a whiff of kibble and realized disappointedly that it wasn't Laurel in the bed beside him.

"Down boy," he commanded both his hard-on and the terrier nuzzling his face.

He cracked open an eyelid. Bright sunlight was streaming in from the high window behind him and Sam had to squint against the pain of it to read the clock on the night stand. Ten-thirty. Slowly, he turned his head toward the hot breath fanning his face. Oreo was indeed lying down, but with his head on his paws and his butt in the air, he looked as if he was likely to spring at Sam any minute.

"Down."

With a frustrated whimper, Oreo settled into the pillow. Sam slowly stretched his weary body. Just as he suspected, Laurel was as impulsive in bed as she was out of it. A slow grin spread over his face just thinking about the things she'd done to him—and he'd done to her—last night. One part of him was up for doing it all over again, but Sam wasn't sure precisely where they stood this morning. Her side of the bed was cold, which meant she was long gone. But she had promised him breakfast and Sam knew exactly how he wanted to break his fast.

Climbing out of bed, he snatched up his clothes off the floor. A framed picture on the wall caught his eye and he paused to study it more closely. It was a charcoal drawing of a landscape that looked a lot like the ranch. Next to it was a stunning painting of a horse racing through the valley. The colors and details were so vivid it looked like a photograph. A black and white sketch of a laughing Tyson sat in a frame on the nightstand. Sam picked it up, carefully scanning the portrait for the initials that were in the corners of the other artwork decorating the room—LEK.

He smiled in wonderment. Laurel was an artist. A good one if he was any judge. That certainly fit her impetuous personality more than a bean counter. It seemed Laurel was quashing more of her true self than he thought.

Oreo was snoring contentedly when Sam made his way to the large, modern bathroom. The room featured a double vanity, a spacious walk-in shower and a vintage claw-foot tub. His junk grew tight just thinking of how he'd bent Laurel over that tub hours earlier. Reaching into the shower, he turned the water to cold. He was going to need it.

When he emerged fifteen minutes later, Laurel was in the kitchen rummaging through the cabinets. She was dressed in her riding uniform of ass-hugging jeans, a bright western shirt, and cowboy boots.

"Hi." There was a wary tone to her voice. Sam hoped like hell it wasn't regret.

"Morning." He shoved his hands in his pockets to keep from reaching for her and kissing the look of uncertainty off her face. Oreo trotted over and sat on Sam's boot.

"Oreo hates strangers. What did you do to him?"

The little dog was gazing up at Sam expectantly while its stumpy tail swished back and forth.

"I'm sure he just misses Tyson," Sam said.

Laurel reached down and patted the dog. "He's having fun without us, little buddy."

The wistful way she said it made something catch in Sam's chest. "How long will Tyson be away?"

"Five days." Her lips trembled before settling into a tenuous smile, as though she was trying to convince herself five days wasn't an eternity.

"Does he spend a lot of time with his dad?"

"They see each other a few times a year," she said. "But Bryce usually comes here. This is the longest I've ever been away from Tyson and, to be honest, I'm not handling it well."

While Sam was relieved her anxiety wasn't morning-after regret, her words stunned him. What father would only see his son "a few times a year"?

"Come here." Sam wrapped his arms around her. He brushed his lips over the soft hair on top of her head and she relaxed against him. "He'll be home before you know it."

"I know. And I keep telling myself that it isn't fair that I have Tyson all to myself every day."

Sam wasn't sure he saw the situation the same way Laurel did. In his opinion, it wasn't fair that she should have all the responsibility of raising her son. Bryce Johnson had gone on with his life, gallivanting all over the world and chasing his dreams while Laurel shouldered the day-to-day burden of caring for Tyson. Based on the artwork in the loft, he suspected she'd given up her own dreams, likely blaming herself for the unplanned pregnancy.

"You've done a great job with him," he reassured her. "He's a cute kid."

Her smile was beaming when she leaned back, her arms still draped around Sam's waist. "Why thank you, Captain Cowboy. Keep up the sweet talk and you'll definitely get lucky again." She stretched up on her toes and kissed him soundly.

He slid his hands down to cup her ass, bringing her in contact with the part of him that wanted to do all the talking.

Her sigh was lusty, but she pulled out of his embrace. "I promised you breakfast. Breakfast *food*," she said with a cheeky grin as though she'd read his mind. "Unfortunately, I hadn't counted on company so our selection is limited to Pop Tarts or Special K. I could go over to my parents' house and raid their fridge if you want something a little more sustentative." She arched an eyebrow in question.

"Only if you don't have the brown sugar cinnamon Pop Tarts."

She smiled broadly again, waving a box in front of him. "Tyson's favorite."

Laurel made him a cup of coffee as they munched on their food and chatted about everything and nothing at the same time. The wistful look that had been dragging her mouth down at the corners was gone. Sam told her about his sisters, their children, and his parents, now retired in North Carolina. Laurel laughed as she shared humorous stories of her childhood, her mom's tenure as mayor of Glacier Creek and her days as a champion rider.

"Why did you stop competing?" Sam asked.

She shrugged. "Horses were always my parents' passion. I loved my competition days—especially because they took me out of Montana—but I had different passions I wanted to pursue."

"Like art?" Sam took a sip from his coffee mug.

"Kind of hard for you not to notice, huh?" She shook her head in exasperation. "My mom ran out of room in her house so she put several pieces in here."

"I'm sure she's proud of you. And she should be. You're very talented."

Most women would have blushed at the compliment, but Laurel accepted it as her due. "Thanks. My art professors still bug me to take it up again, but 'Starving Artist' doesn't go hand in hand with motherhood." She shrugged again. "Maybe when Tyson gets older."

Sam wanted to say more, but Laurel picked up her Stetson and pulled it low over her brows.

"I'm going to take Tabitha out for some training," she said. "She's really progressing well. Would you like to stay and watch?"

The thought of watching his lover ride Becky's horse should have bothered Sam more than it did. The truth was he'd endure just about anything to spend more time with Laurel. The only things awaiting him at the A-frame were boxes of memories he'd like to forget and an empty bed. Sam wanted another night in Laurel's bed.

"Sure," he said. Oreo charged through the door in front of them and they both headed down to the barn.

THE SPRING SUN was warm on Laurel's shoulders as she guided Tabitha through a series of patterns and spins. She squeezed her right thigh firmly against Tabitha's flank so the horse spun counterclockwise three-hundred-sixty degrees while keeping her back pivot foot planted in the sand. The mare's spins were nearly perfect—perhaps the best of any horse Laurel had ever ridden. When they ended up in exactly the same spot as they'd begun, Laurel gave her a big pat.

"She's a little better to her left than her right, but then most horses favor one side over the other. A good rider will be able to camouflage that," she said as Tabitha ambled over to the rail where Sam was sitting, looking sexy as hell with his white shirt billowing in the warm breeze. He'd grabbed a Texas Rangers baseball cap out of his truck and pulled it low on his head, but that only accentuated the square jaw she'd traced her tongue along the night before.

Laurel took a long drink from the bottle of water he handed her, hoping it would cool her off. His intense gaze wasn't helping. She glanced down to the V in her blouse where her skin shimmered with a fine sheen of sweat. Pressing the cold bottle to the spot, Laurel sighed. Sam swore beside her, making her laugh, glad she wasn't the only one feeling the sexual pull.

"There a few other things we need to get smoothed out," Laurel continued. "And she needs to develop a bit more muscle before you start advertising her, but I think another six weeks will be all it takes."

He nodded and his mouth formed a grim line. Tabitha nudged his thigh and Sam reached over to stroke her nose. Laurel cursed herself for being so callous. The mare was his late wife's prized possession and she was nonchalantly talking about selling her.

"Will you miss her?" she asked.

Sam seemed startled by the question. "No. I wasn't around the farm much. I was deployed most of the time Becky had her."

"Tell me about her."

"Tabitha? All her info is in the package I gave your dad. I'm not even sure of her age."

Laurel shook her head. "Not the horse, silly. Your wife. Becky." She wasn't sure why she'd asked the question except that suddenly, knowing this man's body wasn't enough. Laurel wanted to know everything that was Sam Gaskill. And his late wife certainly held some clues.

Sam looked away from her and stared out at the lake as if the answer to her question was buried at the bottom. He was quiet so long that she didn't think he'd answer her.

"Why do women always want to know this shit," he finally said. "What's so important that you want to know about her? She's gone and she's not coming back."

Her stomach squeezed at the annoyed look on his face and her head was telling her to let this go. As usual, her mouth wasn't listening. "Because she's still here. With Tabitha. With you."

He swore violently, sending Oreo and Truman scurrying into the barn. Tabitha shifted from side to side but Laurel refused to be cowed. The laugh he gave had a hollow ring to it. "To hear Becky tell it, I left her years before she left this earth."

Laurel swallowed her gasp. "So you're not 'pining' after the love of your life?" Her mother would be appalled at the indelicacy of the question, but his answer would change how she viewed him. How she viewed *them*.

Sam's stare was hard and challenging. "Only as much as

you're pining after Bryce Johnson."

She didn't bother stopping her quicksilver grin as something warm and fuzzy unfurled inside of her. Dismounting from the horse, she held onto the reins and climbed up onto the fence beside him. Laurel leaned in and brushed her lips against his. Sam responded by wrapping his hands around her head, dislodging her hat in the process, and kissing her with a reckless force that nearly had them toppling off the fence. Digging her fingers in the wood, Laurel let him have his way with her, punishing her with his lips, his tongue, and his teeth.

She groaned when Sam finally nipped at her lip before jumping down and retrieving her hat. He plopped it on her head then settled his back against the wood between Laurel's thighs. She wrapped her arms around his shoulders and leaned in to trace the shell of his ear with her tongue.

"Tell me your story," she urged him.

He let out a frustrated sigh. "Becky was PK—a preacher's kid. I met her on the base. She worked in the battalion office, answering phones and doing other things for the CO."

Laurel began gently kneading his tight shoulders and Sam draped his arms over her thighs.

He relaxed beneath her hands as he continued. "It's the usual tale told around every military base in the world. I was shipping out to face God-knows-what. At twenty-three, I thought I knew shit, that I had it all figured out, but really I was a green kid. I wanted someone to write to me, to keep me connected with what was going on here in the States. Something to look forward to. Becky just wanted out of her daddy's house." He was quiet again, and Laurel massaged the back of his neck until he spoke once more. "My parents, my sisters, they all have these amazing marriages. I was too ashamed to let anyone know I'd made a mistake. It wasn't Becky. She was a really sweet girl. I think maybe if we'd had kids. . ."

His voice trailed off, and suddenly Laurel's shoulders ached, too.

"I bought Tabitha for her so she'd have something to do when I went on my second deployment. The horse made her happy."

And likely made you feel less guilty, Laurel thought. Her chest was aching along with her shoulders.

"How did she die?" Laurel asked softly.

Sam's body tensed up again. "We'd had a fight. I told her I was re-upping for one more tour and she was not happy. She hated what I did for a living. Despite the distance in our marriage, she didn't want me to leave again. Funny, since she hated having me around. It kept her from spending time with Tabitha." He reached over and tugged on the horse's ear. "Becky took off in a rage. She took Tabitha up into Hill Country. They were both familiar with the trails there, but somehow Becky came off."

Tears burned the back of Laurel's eyes. She hated where

this was going, knowing Sam felt guilt for something that was not his fault.

"She hit her head and bled out before we found her. I didn't know she was pregnant until the autopsy."

The breath seized in Laurel's chest and her fingers stilled on Sam's neck. He'd lost his wife *and a child.*

"Was the baby yours?" Laurel chewed on her lip, anticipating his reaction.

Sam surprised the hell out of her by laughing. "Only you would ask that out loud."

He turned around to face her, letting his hands span her waist.

She cupped his chin. "I really do try to control it."

His grin was resigned. "Becky wasn't that kind of woman, no matter how unhappy she was. The baby was mine. DNA evidence doesn't lie."

"I'm sorry," she said before leaning down and brushing a kiss along his jaw.

"Mmm," he said. "It's in the past. All that's left is to make sure her horse is taken care of."

Laurel patted Tabitha on the neck. She doubted being free of the mare would absolve Sam of the guilt he was carrying around, but she'd do her best to see that Tabitha went to a rider who had a shot at the championship.

Sam's eyes had that hot and hungry look in them again. "You never told me what you noticed first about me?" Clearly Sam wanted a subject change.

Laurel stepped down from her perch on the fence, sliding her body against his as she did. Trying for a seductive smile, she slid her fingers into the back pockets of his jeans and gripped his firm ass. "Your eyes," she answered. "They were sad when you weren't glowering and they made me want to do this." And then she kissed him.

EARLY THE NEXT morning, Laurel studied Sam as he lay sleeping naked in the bed beside her. He was so beautiful with his chiseled muscles, lush eyelashes, and kissable lips. Even better, he was a generous lover, always taking his time to make sure she was satisfied. Not that her satisfaction took that much time to achieve given his talented hands and mouth. She smiled smugly to herself, pleased she'd been lucky enough to have ended her sexual drought with a guy like Sam.

They'd spent the previous day wandering the ranch with Oreo and Truman in tow. Laurel wasn't sure how long they'd hiked before she'd noticed that Sam's hand had slipped easily around hers. Somehow, his fingers threaded through hers felt more intimate than when his body was inside her. The thought was both calming and unnerving at the same time.

While Laurel liked the idea of their physical closeness, it was the mental connection that ruffled her. He seemed to know her—*to get her*—like no one else did. Sam didn't chastise her impulsiveness. Instead, he embraced it as one of the many facets of her. His acceptance was freeing. Laurel felt like a light-headed high school girl again.

She'd even acted like a high school girl, lying to Ivy about why she couldn't meet for dinner last night. But she didn't want to share what she had with Sam yet. Not when she wasn't sure what she wanted with him.

Now gazing at him unabashedly, she felt a stirring of sadness that his face didn't relax even in sleep. Whether it was his experiences in war, with Becky, or something else, Sam's body couldn't seem to let go of all the tension coiling within it. Given that her own body felt like a rag doll's after spending the past thirty-six hours in some form of sexual encounter with the man, the strain gripping him troubled her.

And the idea that she was concerned about him could only mean one thing. She was falling for the guy. A man who risked his life for a living. *Damn it.* She flopped onto her back and blew out a breath. This was why she needed to curb her impulsiveness.

"Woman, your sexual appetite is insatiable." His profile was unchanged except for a slight uptick of the corners of his lips. "Don't get me wrong, I'm happy to oblige. But do you have to wake up so damn early every morning?"

She rolled back over so that her bare flesh brushed up against his. He hissed slightly when her hand found his arousal beneath the sheets. "The day starts early on a ranch.

There are chores to do and horses to ride."

His eyelids gradually lifted, and that amber gaze of his was so arresting, the breath got hung up in Laurel's chest.

"Now that you mention it, an invigorating morning ride sounds like a pretty good idea," he murmured before pulling her on top of him.

Laurel's worries about her vulnerable heart melted away when her lips met his. *This was all that mattered right now.* She'd concentrate on enjoying this man and taking away some of the stress that weighed him down. Everything else could wait until real life returned tomorrow. Their bodies began the now familiar dance and Laurel lost herself in the sheer bliss of it.

Later, she lay sated and sprawled out on Sam's chest as he gently dragged his fingers through her hair. His heart was still pounding beneath her palm.

"I'm gonna need more than a Pop Tart after that," he said. "I knew I should have grabbed those breakfast burritos from my freezer when I went home yesterday to get a change of clothes."

She wrinkled her nose at him. "I think we can do better than frozen food. How about breakfast in town? I'm pretty sure I can get us a table for brunch at Cady's."

His hand stilled in her hair. "You want to take this public?"

Laurel wasn't sure what she wanted. She wasn't even sure what 'this' was. But she did know while she'd ended her drought, she'd clearly begun something else. And she wasn't ready to for it to end.

She rested her chin on her hands that were pressed against his chest and met his gaze. "Are you afraid to be seen with me, Captain Cowboy?"

One of his eyebrows shot up. "Afraid to be seen with Glacier Creek High School's Miss Congeniality? Hell, no. My reputation could use the boost."

"It'll just be two people having breakfast." She reminded herself as much as Sam.

He nodded solemnly. "I like what I do with my life, Laurel. That's not going to change."

"I repeat, just breakfast, Captain Cowboy." Laurel was proud of her ability to remain cool in spite of the fact that her insides were shouting at her to end things now before she got in too deep.

"I like this, too," he said softly before leaning in to kiss the tip of her nose. "A lot."

Laurel liked it a lot, too, which was precisely why she was ignoring her insides. She rolled off him, hoping the loss of contact between their bodies would help refocus her head.

"I just need to check in with Bryce first. I want to talk to Tyson before they head out to the park for the day."

"Sure. I'll get the shower warmed up."

Sam climbed out of bed and headed toward the bathroom. Laurel paused as she dialed her phone to admire the perfection that was Sam's naked ass. When he stopped at the kitchen and poured some food in Oreo's bowl, Laurel realized she was in big trouble. The man prowling through her loft was more than just a sexy ass. And that was probably what she was attracted to the most.

CHAPTER SEVEN

"**W**HAT'S THE OVER-UNDER on this crop of rookies, Cap?" Hugh Ferguson called to Sam from behind the bar.

The man was filling pitchers of beer for the rowdy crowd that had assembled at The Drop Zone. Apparently, it was a tradition in Glacier Creek for everyone to celebrate the men and women who survived the first day of rookie camp with a beer and a fish fry at the local tavern. It was barely five o'clock on a Monday and it seemed like most of the town had crammed into the bar. Sam had to give Hugh Ferguson his due for being not only a top notch smokejumper, but a marketing genius as well.

Sam glanced toward the back of the room where the twelve men and three women were being congratulated for passing the initial PT unit. Although, he wasn't sure the rookies should be celebrating just yet. The forest service's requirement of seven pull-ups, twenty-five push-ups, forty-five sit-ups, and a one-and-one-half mile run in under eleven minutes was a cake walk compared to what they'd face during the brutal four-week camp, much less the actual four to five month fire season.

"You know as well as I do that the odds are only five or six will make it to the end of the month," Sam said. "But there's a lot of talent in that bunch. I'm confident that between this rookie class and the part-time staff we'll have the right crew when the season starts."

"Pfeiffer will drop out by Thursday," Ferguson said as he pulled the cork from a wine bottle and poured Chardonnay into two glasses. "He tries out every year but never gets past the first pack out. Last year, he was screaming like a girl at the tree climb. I swear he only comes to camp to get laid by the smokejumper groupies."

Sure enough, the bulky firefighter in question had a harem of young women surrounding him, hanging on his every word. Sam grinned as he lifted his bottle of beer to his lips. "Hey, you can't blame a guy for using every tool in the shed."

Hugh scoffed as he headed down the bar, the two wine glasses in his hand. "If you're lucky some poor woman will marry his ass before he ages out."

"Who's Uncle Hugh marrying off now?"

Laurel slipped in between two barstools, her body brushing up against Sam's as she propped her elbows behind her on top of the wooden bar and leaned back so that she had a clear view of the rest of the room. Sam let out a slow, agonized breath at the sight of her. It had been over twenty-four hours since he'd last been near her—last touched her—

and his body was feeling every second of their separation.

The frilly, yellow sundress she wore swirled around her knees when she moved. A perfect white pearl tethered to a leather band swayed provocatively from side to side just above the valley between her breasts. When Laurel hooked the heel of her boot on the rail at the base of the wooden bar, one of the skimpy straps of her dress slid down her shoulder. Sam didn't bother checking his movements. He reached out and slowly pushed the strap back up, allowing his finger to trail along her smooth skin as he did. Laurel watched him through the fringes of her eyelashes, her lips seeming to part on a sigh.

It was a bold, proprietary statement in front of most of the town, but Sam didn't give a shit. He wanted everyone to know they were involved. More importantly, he wanted Laurel to know it. She was still hung up on him being a smokejumper, he got that. But this wasn't about marriage and a white picket fence. This was about two people enjoying each other's company in an adult, no-strings-attached relationship for as long as it lasted.

At least that was what he kept telling himself.

She slowly lifted her gaze from his finger that was still loitering on her shoulder to study his face. "Someone's getting married?" The breathless way she asked the question made his body grow hard.

Reluctantly, Sam pulled his hand away from her warm skin. "No. Just wishful thinking on your uncle's part about

Pfeiffer."

She laughed. "Pfeiffer hasn't given up yet? How many pull-ups did he manage this year?"

"He eked out the seven he needed."

Laurel's eyes seemed to be fixated on his chest while she chewed on her plump bottom lip. "How many can you do, Captain Cowboy?"

Sam swallowed a long sip of beer in order to quench his suddenly dry mouth. "I did twenty-four this morning."

Her chin jerked up and Sam was surprised at the heat in her green eyes. "I'll just bet you did." Her smile was a bit smug. "I'm sure you enjoyed showing off in front of your team and the new recruits. I hope you didn't let anyone best you."

He took another pull from his beer before answering. "Dodson got twenty-five."

Laurel's gasp sounded more like a laugh. "I have to say I'm surprised, but then, Tyler is a bit of a stud."

Jealousy, hot and sharp, licked at Sam's gut at the thought of Laurel ogling Tyler Dodson while he flaunted his washboard abs at the pull-up bar this morning. Kingston had been the first to shed his shirt, throwing it down in challenge when there were only five remaining in the competition. Clark, Ferguson, and Dodson had followed suit, causing a chant among the rest of the crowd for Sam to do the same.

Laurel had been right. Sam had something to prove, not only to the rookies, but to the team serving under him.

Answering their challenge, Sam had yanked off his shirt and tossed it on the pile. The five of them took to the bars, flexing their muscles and showing the rookies and everyone else what kind of strength it took to be a smokejumper. And when it was over, Tyler had nudged Sam by one.

"I let him win."

This time her laughter rang out across the room as she tossed her head back to let the sound escape. That pulse was beating wildly at her neck again and Sam wrapped his fingers more tightly around his bottle of beer to keep from touching her there.

"I would have liked to have seen that," she said, her eyes drifting to his chest again. She'd likely already heard all about the testosterone-fueled exhibition from her cousin, Miranda, Sam realized too late. "I'm sure you had a good reason to let Tyler beat you."

He had. One of the trainers, a hard-ass former smoke-jumper, had been berating Dodson from the minute he'd stepped on base that morning. It was only after inquiring of Jacqui Edwards that Sam learned the guy was Dodson's stepfather. It irked Sam that, even as adults, the guy would try to belittle his own family. "Mike Eldridge was being an ass to him."

Laurel's face softened and she turned and linked her arm through his. "So, you're a big softy with people as well as dogs." She gave his arm a squeeze and Sam suddenly wished they were anywhere but this crowded bar. "There's a lot of history there. Mike can be a prickly jerk to his stepson. Russ used to act as a buffer between them. I'm glad you've stepped into Russ's shoes. I'm pretty sure Tyler feels the same way, Captain Cowboy." She lowered her voice to a whisper. "I wouldn't let Tyler in on your secret, though. He's got a lot of pride packed into those sexy muscles."

A bartender slid a plate of nachos and Laurel's white wine toward Sam. He was glad for the distraction because he didn't want Laurel thinking about Dodson's damn muscles. She reached over to snag a chip off the plate, but Sam pulled it away.

"You're not going to share?" She gaped at him incredulously.

"I'll share my nachos, Laurel. But I'm done sharing you."

Her lips closed and her eyes grew stormy, but Sam didn't give her time to protest. He handed her his beer and her wine and turned her toward the crowd. Grabbing the plate of nachos, he took her elbow and guided her through the maze of tables toward a spot in the back corner of the bar. Partially obscured by a parachute canopy that had likely belonged to Hugh at one time, the table suited his purpose of privacy.

Unfortunately, his plan was botched by one of the rookies—Sam couldn't for the life of him remember the guy's name—who was already at the table shoveling down a piece from one of the cakes the local bakery had donated for the evening. He paused with his fork halfway to his mouth, his eyes wide as Sam pinned him with a stare that he'd perfected on mouthy corporals in Afghanistan.

"Hey, Cap," the guy murmured before his eyes darted to Laurel. "Uh, here, why don't you take this seat. I'm headed home to catch a few Zs before tomorrow, anyway." He swiped at the table with a napkin and skirted around Laurel, making his way to the front of the bar. "I'll see you in the morning, captain. Sir."

Laurel shook her head as she put the wine and beer down on the table. "Was that really necessary?"

Sam placed the plate of nachos on the table and pulled Laurel's body against his. "Hell, yeah," he growled.

Nudging her with his hips, he pressed her into the darkened corner as he seized her mouth in a deep, searching kiss. His hands found her ass through the thin cotton of her dress. The blood rushed from his brain to his crotch when her body arched into his.

He felt her start to resist, but then just as suddenly she was sliding her tongue against his, opening her mouth wider to give him better access. Sam wedged a thigh between her legs and she bucked. In return, Laurel fisted her fingers in his shirt seemingly trying to close the miniscule distance between their bodies. The noise from the bar faded away until all Sam could hear were the deep sounds of need coming from the back of her throat.

"I missed you," she whispered when he broke the kiss to explore her neck. "The loft was lonely with only Oreo's snoring to keep me company."

"Let's skip the damn nachos and go back to your place," Sam said as his brushed his lips along her jaw.

Laurel sighed. "I. . .we can't. My parents are there. I shouldn't even be here. I'd planned on studying tonight." She balled her hands into fists and thumped his chest. "Instead I'm doing this. With you. Again."

Sam chuckled as he pressed a kiss to her forehead. "Because you like 'this' too much."

She punched his chest again. "I'm still trying to figure out what 'this' is."

"Damn it, it doesn't have to *be* anything other than sex. Really great sex, I might add."

She pulled out of their embrace and wrapped her arms tightly around her middle. A strand of hair had fallen into her face and she blew at it with lips that were still puffy from his kisses. "If you were really that type of guy, you would have moved on by now."

Sam took a step back, trying to focus on her words while still mesmerized by her mouth. Sighing heavily, he dragged his fingers through his hair. She was right, he wasn't that type of guy, but he damn sure wanted to be. Life was a hell of a lot easier without putting his heart on the line. He'd learned that one the hard way. Women always had to complicate things, to pick apart everything, and talk about it until there was nothing left of a guy's heart but one of those hollow, empty cardboard valentine boxes.

Damn, how Sam wanted to prove Laurel wrong and be that guy who moved on, who took sex without giving anything in return but toe-curling orgasms. But when he met her gaze, Laurel's normally spirited eyes were damp and wary. Something speared in his chest, making him swear beneath his breath again.

"I should go," she said softly.

He should let her go. Let *this* go. But he couldn't. The pull with her was too great. Sam wasn't going to change what he was, but he wasn't above enjoying whatever scraps she threw his way before the bone-weary months of the fire season chewed him up and spit him out.

"Stay. Eat something. Finish your wine. You can't study on an empty stomach."

Laurel gnawed on her bottom lip. Sam reached behind her and pulled out her chair. "Sit," he commanded. "I promise to keep my hands to myself."

She sat down with a disappointed huff. "Well that's not really an inducement."

He laughed as he slid into his own chair. "I can always count on you to speak your mind."

"It's my greatest handicap." Her eyes met his as she stared at him over the rim of her wine glass. "Well, one of them anyway."

Sam leaned back in his chair as she sipped her wine. He pulled a nacho off the plate and crunched it, trying to tamp down on his rising frustration. "Is that how you see me? As a handicap?"

"No! I'm sorry, I didn't mean that." She reached across the table and took his hand in hers. "If anything, I'm the one who's handicapped. I keep picking guys who…who…" She chewed on her lip again.

Damn it, this one time why couldn't she say what she meant?

"Who what, Laurel?"

"Who—"

Her friend, the woman with blonde ringlets, the big blue eyes, and an insatiable thirst for appletinis, stepped around the parachute. "Laurel?"

Laurel tried to pull her hand free, but Sam wrapped his fingers around hers and held on. She shot him an aggravated look before turning to her friend. "Ivy? What's up?"

Ivy's gaze bounced from Laurel to Sam and back again. "Um, Bryce is here."

Her hand went limp in his grasp. "What? Bryce is where?"

"Here," a male voice said as Ivy stepped away to reveal Bryce Johnson and his cheesy grin.

ALL THE AIR seemed to leave Laurel's lungs in one gasp. "Bryce! What are you doing here?" Panic suddenly set in and she glanced past Bryce and Ivy. "Where's Tyson?"

She tugged at her hand, anxious to look in the front of

the bar for Tyson. But Sam wouldn't let go. Didn't he understand that something must be wrong with her son and she needed to get to him? Laurel glared at him, but when she met Sam's eyes, a fierce determination shone back at her. There was compassion in them, too, but what hit her hardest was the calm competence she saw reflected there. The reliable soldier that was ingrained in him. He was there for her, his eyes communicated, soothing her. With a slight nod, he slowly released her fingers.

"Relax, Tyson's fine," Bryce said as he helped himself to a nacho. "He's at home with your parents."

Confused, Laurel's heart was still racing. "I don't understand. You weren't supposed to be home until tomorrow."

"Change in plans." Bryce wiped his hands with a napkin and fixed his gaze on Sam. "Sorry to put a monkey wrench in *your* plans, though."

Ivy giggled before quickly covering it with a feigned cough. Her friend shot an apologetic look at Laurel. It belatedly registered with Laurel that they weren't alone. Worse, the crowded bar had quieted substantially. *All the better to eavesdrop on what was playing out behind Hugh's parachute.* Her stomach rolled. It wasn't enough that everyone in town gossiped about her being a single mother with a superstar baby daddy. Now Bryce was making it seem as though she was out partying and hooking up while Tyson was away.

Which, of course, she was, *damn it.*

"You must be the soldier Tyson was talking about." Bryce extended his hand toward Sam. "The one with the...*horse* Laurel is riding."

Laurel cringed at the double entendre, her anger with Bryce escalating. His hand hung in the air awkwardly for a long moment before Sam grasped it with his own. "Yep," was all he said. He was a mountain of unflinching muscle as he stared Bryce down.

Tori, seemingly oblivious of the palpable tension, slipped in between Ivy and Bryce. "On the house," she said with her mouth while her hips communicated a host of invitations.

Bryce accepted the bottle of Blue Moon with the trademark smile his parents had paid a fortune to a Marin County dentist for.

"Thank you, darlin'."

"Whatever you want," Tori called over her shoulder with a wink.

Ivy crossed her arms in front of her and groaned audibly. Laurel would have, too, but she still wasn't sure what was happening.

"Bryce, tell me what's going on. Now," she ordered. It wasn't lost on her that she had to use the same mommy voice she used with Tyson on a grown man. "Why are you home early? Tyson was looking forward to this trip. What happened?"

"That's the thing," Bryce said sheepishly. "I don't think he was ready for a trip like this."

"What do you mean?" she demanded.

"He's kind of whiny and a bit of a baby."

"What?" Laurel stared at Bryce in disbelief.

"He's *five!*" Ivy shouted.

"Going on six. And you two"—Bryce pointed to Ivy before turning his finger on Laurel—"have turned him into a mama's boy."

Laurel would have charged across the table, but Sam's hand on her arm stopped her. He gave her that look again and she sucked in a deep breath.

"It's the first time the boy had been away from his mother for any length of time, Johnson. It happens," Sam said quietly. "If you spent some time with him, you'd see he's a typical kid who is, in fact, very independent."

Bryce's body stiffened and the people in the bar seemed to collectively hold their breath while Garth Brooks sang about friends in low places on the jukebox.

"Well, well, Laurel." Bryce's eyes grew hard as he directed his stare at Sam. "It seems this guy knows more about my son than I do. Is there something you're not telling me about your relationship with the captain?"

She buried her head in her hands with a groan. "There is no relationship!"

Sam stilled beside her, and even the stupid jukebox was quiet as it shifted to a new song. Laurel peeked out from behind her fingers to see Ivy, her eyes wide in her pale face. Bryce, on the other hand, wore a cocky expression that clearly said he was having fun stirring up trouble. The thing with Bryce was that he thought everyone wanted to push the envelope like he did. He didn't understand there were repercussions to most of his bold words or actions. Bryce was a lot like his five-year-old son that way.

She was saved from having to look at Sam when the sound of alarms sounded on multiple cell phones.

"Cap?" Miranda poked her head around the parachute. "The crash site is seventy miles west of here. Because we're going that direction we've got an hour and a half left of daylight. I can be wheels up in twenty minutes and have you on scene in forty-five."

Sam looked up from the screen of his phone just as Tyler Dodson rounded the corner. "I need three people to suit up," Sam told Tyler in that no-nonsense military tone of his. "We'll go in with search and rescue and make sure the fire stays contained. It'll be boots out though, so we'll be gone overnight at the very least."

"Ferguson and Rivers are gearing up in the ready room now. I'll be your fourth."

Laurel shivered at the cavalier way Tyler put his life on the line, as though he were simply committing himself to a game of cards.

"Let's go," Sam said.

It stupidly dawned on her that Sam was going, too. He wasn't issuing orders to a crew; he was leading it.

Jumping from an airplane into a fire.

"Wait!" Laurel shot out of her chair, barely able to squeeze the word out through her constricting throat.

She'd hurt him a moment ago. Not that he'd ever admit it. But she knew she had. This thing between them confused him just as much as it did Laurel. She needed to apologize, to fix this, in case...in case... She swallowed roughly, unwilling to fathom what might happen to him.

Sam's body was poised for flight and she could see it was costing him to halt. When he turned toward her, his eyes still had that steely, competent look, but the compassion that had been there moments earlier was gone. Laurel's felt its loss down to her toes.

The Dixie Chicks were singing something about things not working out and Laurel would have laughed at the irony—except tears burned the back of her eyes.

"I—you—I," she stammered.

"Laurel," Sam said, not bothering to conceal his impatience. "A small plane has crashed into the side of a mountain. There are three people who need to be rescued and a fire that needs to be contained. Whatever this is, it's going to have to wait."

He was right. She felt foolish and small and just a little bit desperate, emotions she'd sworn never to feel again after she'd first become pregnant with Tyson. But now wasn't the time for her and Sam to resolve things.

"Of course, yes." She nodded, tucking her trembling hands behind her.

Just when he looked like he might say something more, he turned and headed out of the bar.

"Be safe," she whispered at his retreating back.

Miranda gave her a sympathetic look before hurrying after Sam.

CHAPTER EIGHT

"**W**HAT DO YOU mean you didn't tell Tyson you're getting married?" Laurel had just gotten her emotions under control when Bryce dropped yet another bombshell.

Earlier, she'd hurried from the bar, eager to get back to the ranch and see for herself that her son was in fact fine. It wasn't until Tyson had wrapped his skinny arms around her neck and she'd breathed in that familiar scent of sweaty little boy and baby shampoo that she felt her chest begin to relax a bit.

"I missed you," she whispered against the smooth skin of his cheek.

"I missed everyone," Tyson said, his blue eyes shining when Laurel brushed his soft hair off his face. "But I missed you the most."

Laurel managed a painful swallow; her throat was so constricted with emotion. "Didn't you have fun meeting Mickey and Donald?"

"Yeah, but I wanted you to meet them, too."

She hugged him more tightly as she squeezed her eyes

shut to hold back tears.

A half hour later, dusk was falling at the ranch. Seated in his grandmother's lap on the big porch of the main house with Oreo, Truman, and Pirate crowded at his feet, Tyson was busy telling all the animals about his trip. Laurel and Bryce had wandered over to one of the paddocks to speak more privately.

"I tried to tell him about the wedding, believe me, but he refused to give Audrianna more than two words the entire time. I think he was a little put out that she was even there," Bryce explained.

"He doesn't get a lot of time with just you."

Bryce rested his forearms on the wooden fence. "Don't hit me with a guilt trip, Laurel. You know what my life is like. Full-time fatherhood was never in the Olympic training plan."

Her sigh was part exasperation and part guilt. "I know that, Bryce. And for the millionth time, I'm sorry."

Bryce swore. "Stop it. I don't regret having a son. And I certainly don't regret that you're his mother. I wish things could have worked out between us, but they didn't. Tyson needs to fit into the life I'm making, though, Laurel."

Laurel wrapped her arms around her middle in hopes of quelling the rising nausea that this conversation always brought on. "He's in kindergarten. He doesn't understand everything that's happening. Give him time."

"I'm not sure time is going to change the scenario that

Tyson has in his head."

She cringed, thinking about what Sam said Tyson had told him the previous week. Laurel had ignored it, not wanting to put a damper on her son's trip. Now she wondered if she'd just been in as much denial as her son.

"Mommy! Daddy," Tyson called merrily as he ran from the porch, Oreo barking excitedly at his heels. "Grandpa says there are new baby lambs at the animal sanctuary. Can we go see them tomorrow? Please?" He scrambled up on the railing between Laurel and Bryce and wrapped an arm around them both. "Maybe Daddy could take me to school in the morning tomorrow. Cameron's daddy drops him off in the mornings so his mommy can sleep in. Mommy has been studying a lot. We should let her sleep in, huh, Daddy?" Tyson chattered on while Bryce looked shell-shocked. "Then we can all have a family outing to the sanctuary. There are picnic tables and a playground. Lots of families have picnics there."

Bryce's blue eyes—so much like Tyson's—had that 'I told you so' look in them when they met hers over the top of their son's head.

"Tyson, honey," Laurel said gently. "Nobody's sleeping in tomorrow because I have to work and you'll want to go to school and tell Miss Ivy and your friends about Disneyland." She went for a diversion, peering into Tyson's ear. "Oh, my goodness, I think I see some pixie dust that Tinker Bell must have left in your ears," she teased. "How about we get you into the tub?"

Her son wasn't easily distracted, however. He wrapped his arms firmly around Bryce's neck. "Daddy can give me a bath. I want to show him my wind-up hippo toy."

When Bryce didn't immediately respond, Laurel stepped in, just as she always did. "Honey, Daddy can't stay. You can show him your toy another time." She said a silent prayer her son would understand.

Tyson's eyes dimmed. "Can't you stay until the little hand is on the nine?" he asked softly.

Bryce shifted Tyson in his arms so the two were nose to nose. "Remember how I told you that I have to go to find the snow so I can practice for the Olympics?"

Tyson's head bobbed up and down solemnly.

"Well, the team is leaving for South America soon and I have to get my gear all ready. I have to fly back to Utah tonight."

"They have rain forests in South America. Did you know that, Daddy?"

Bryce's face softened as he gazed in amazement at their son. "I did know that, Halfpipe."

"The horned frogs live there. We learned about them in school."

"Should I bring you one back?" Bryce had that devilish gleam in his eyes again and Laurel swiftly shook her head behind Tyson's. The situation was bad enough without Bryce making all kinds of promises he couldn't likely keep.

"Yes!" Tyson wrapped his arms around his father's neck. Bryce smiled smugly, oblivious that he'd just set his son up for yet another disappointment.

"You behave for your mama okay, Halfpipe?" Bryce tickled Tyson as he let him slide down.

Laurel's mother called to Tyson. "Sweetie, why don't you come have a bath in Grandma's Jacuzzi tub. You can finish telling me about riding the monorail."

Tyson squeezed his father around the knees while Bryce ruffled his hair. "I can't wait until the 'lympics is over, Daddy. Then we can all be together every day," he said before racing off toward the house.

Bryce swore again before angrily yanking the keys to his rental car out of his pants pocket.

"I'm sorry." Laurel hated how she always seemed to be saying that to Bryce. "I honestly didn't know he ever considered that a reality. I should have nipped it in the bud last week when he said something similar to Sam."

He eyed her skeptically. "Soldier Sam seems to know a lot about our son."

"They barely know one another," she said, a tad too defensively.

"And how well do *you* know the good soldier?"

"None of your business."

"I have a right to know if the guy is going to be hanging around Tyson," he said sharply.

Laurel glared at him over the hood of his rental car.

"Funny, I never used that excuse to pry about your legion of snow bunnies."

His eyes narrowed. "Audrianna is the only woman I've introduced our son to. And that's because he'll be seeing her for the rest of his life."

She didn't bother commenting that the bookies weren't giving very good odds that Bryce and Audrianna's marriage would have that type of longevity. "There's nothing between Sam and me," she lied.

Only because she couldn't define what exactly there was between them. Great sex, certainly. But even if she could get over Sam risking his life every day, she wasn't sure it could ever be a *rest of their lifetime* relationship, either. Sam had made it clear he wasn't looking for anything long-term. Not that Bryce needed to know any of those details.

He studied her with a critical gaze for a long moment. "Too bad," he finally said.

Laurel rocked back on her heels. "Excuse me?"

Bryce heaved a sigh before dragging his fingers through his hair. "Jesus, Laurel, do you think this is easy for me?" He spun around, gesturing wildly at the ranch surrounding them. "Your dream was to get out of here. To become a commercial artist. To see the world. Instead, you're right back where you started. Crunching numbers in this wild west town. With a kid to boot. *My kid.* Do you think I'm that cold that I don't want to see you happy? With someone?"

Stunned, Laurel shivered slightly in the evening air. Bryce had honored her wish to keep their child, never once holding it against her. He paid his share and then some. And she knew he loved their son. But she also knew him well enough to know his outburst was as much about alleviating his guilt so he could go on with his life unscathed as it was about making her feel better. Although he hadn't meant his words to wound, they did.

His expression shifted from aggravated to sheepish. "Look, I've got to go or I won't make my flight. Can you— can you just tell him about Audrianna and me before the news is all over the Internet?"

"No." Laurel kept her own face steely. "I'm happy to explain to him that there is no way in hell we are ever going to be a normal family with the three of us living happily ever after. But I think the news about your wedding should come from you. He'll need reassurance that he's going to still be a part of your life."

"This shouldn't be so damn hard, Laurel," he argued.

"Parenting is hard, Bryce. I don't make you do it that often. And it's not like you'll be around dealing with the aftermath."

"Fine." She could tell by the way he ground the word out it wasn't fine, but she really didn't care. "I'll come back next month with Audrianna and we'll tell him together. Make sure you live up to your part of the bargain, though. I don't want those crazy thoughts still in his head when I get back from South America." He slid into the driver's side of the car. "Let my assistant know if Tyson needs anything while I'm gone."

"I hope your assistant can get an endangered horn toad out of the Amazon rain forest," she said just to be contrary.

His shoulders slumped. "Do you think he'll be satisfied with a stuffed one?"

The fire seemed to fizzle out of her and she didn't have it in her to continue taunting him. "Sure."

Bryce closed the car door and started up the engine. "Take care of yourself, Laurel," he said through the open window. "I'm glad that you're at least riding again. You were too good of an athlete to just let your competitive edge fizzle away. Try and have some fun while you're at it." He treated her to that amazing smile of his, the one that had gotten her into so much trouble in the first place, and with a jaunty wave, he was gone.

For the second time that night a man had left her behind, wondering what she was doing with her life. She wandered into the soothing confines of the barn. Night was falling and the flute-like singing of the western meadowlark was fading out as the owls took over the evening chorus. The barn was quiet, except for the whir of the overhead fans and a cricket complaining somewhere among the bales of hay. Tabitha was standing solemnly in the corner of her stall, her head relaxed and her eyes partially hidden behind her long lashes.

Laurel leaned her elbows on top of the stall door and peered over at the dozing mare. Her stomach instantly knotted up again at the thought of Sam somewhere in the mountains fighting a fire. Despite knowing he was doing what he'd been trained to do, it didn't stop her from worrying about him. About the entire team. She also envied his dedication and drive. Sam and Bryce were doing things they loved. Sure, they were both adrenaline junkies, but at least Sam's work had a purpose.

She hated how she and Sam had parted earlier. They needed to talk, to clear things up. As much as they were attracted to one another, Laurel couldn't allow their relationship to continue, though. She told herself it was because she couldn't chance Tyson getting attached to a guy who risked his life every day. But she was beginning to realize that she couldn't take that chance with her own heart. Especially when all Sam was prepared to offer was sex.

Tabitha ambled over and nuzzled Laurel's arm.

"Your last owner really did a number on him, didn't she?"

The mare sighed, its warm breath tickling Laurel's skin. Leaning in, she nuzzled the horse's neck. "Well, if I can't give him my heart the least I can do is give you a decent shot at winning. You're getting fitter by the day. Tomorrow, we begin the real training."

SAM RAN HIS bare hands over the charred wood checking for any residual heat. By the time they'd reached the crash site twelve hours earlier, three acres of dense forest had been engulfed in a fire ignited by the plane's fuel tanks. The pilot had been unconscious, but his two passengers were able to pull him to safety before the plane exploded. All three had injuries but none were life-threatening. While the two search and rescue crewmembers triaged the wounded and airlifted them out, Sam and his team had circled the fire, stirring it up by digging trenches and chopping out the brush to eliminate any possible fuel that would allow it to spread. Fortunately, the night air was calm and the fire was extinguished just before dawn.

Molly Rivers was hunched over to Sam's right, her palms turning black as she skimmed the ash and timber. "Everything to the east is cool." She straightened up, arching her back into her hands. "Ouch. This has got to be my least favorite part."

Sam got to his feet and wiped his hands together, trying to loosen some of the soot free. Hand feeling the fire was backbreaking and exhausting, but it was critical to ensuring that a fire site was safe. "We still have to pack out ten miles with no trail. You sure that won't be your least favorite part?"

"Are you kidding? It's a gorgeous day in the Rocky Mountains. Most of my young, professional friends are spending it behind a desk. Me? I get to go hiking." She grinned. "Best of all, my boyfriend is waiting at the end of the hike to rub my feet."

On the other side of Sam, Ferguson laughed as he stowed his kombi shovel into one of the cardboard packs the crew would carry out. "The guy is a vet with his hand up some animal's ass all day. Are you sure you want to let him touch you?"

She tsked at Ferguson. "What's the matter Liam? Won't any of the girls in town let you rub their feet?"

Dodson pulled some MRE's from the pack filled with supplies and handed one to Sam. "Molly, didn't you know the reason Liam lives at home is so his mama can protect him from all the women in Montana who want to rub *his* feet?"

"See, and I heard it's because his mama serves him breakfast in bed," Rivers teased as she took her own MRE from Dodson.

Ferguson gave them both a middle finger salute before pulling out his camp stool and tucking into his MRE. He ripped open the pouch containing the entrée and put it inside the plastic bag that contained the chemical heater. Then, he poured a small amount of water in to activate the chemicals before returning the bag back to the cardboard MRE box for a few minutes, allowing it to heat up.

"Not that I wouldn't kill either of you two for one of my mother's biscuits right now," Ferguson grumbled after swallowing a few bites of the pasta meal. "*This* is the worst part of the job, Molly."

Molly reached into her own pack and pulled out several power bars. She tossed one to each of the men sitting with her. "Who loves me now, boys?"

Sam relaxed at the sound of his team's banter. They were all a bit punchy after the long night of grueling work, but Sam was pleased at how efficiently the firefighters had gotten the job done. Even with the added complication of casualties, they'd managed to contain the blaze quickly and professionally.

"Any word from base on the pilot and passengers?" Dodson asked.

"I asked search and rescue to give Jacqui an update when they got back." Sam glanced at his watch. "I know you all want to linger over this gourmet breakfast, but there's at least eight hours between me and a hot shower and I'd like to get a move on."

Ferguson shot to his feet. "You don't have to tell me twice, Cap. Tonight is karaoke night at The Drop Zone."

Molly groaned as she pulled her pack over her shoulders. "I don't suppose that means you'll be saving your voice so we can be zen with nature on the way out?"

"Come on, Molls, you love when I get my Adam Levine on."

She laughed. "Your singing voice is enhanced by the copious amount of alcohol your father serves. But I have to admit, when you start shaking your butt, it's pretty hot."

Ferguson shook his ass in front of her and Rivers

groaned.

"Hey, why don't you move that ass to the back of the line?" Sam picked up his pulaski and began wielding it like a machete as he and Dodson carved out a trail through the woods. The work was mind-numbingly distracting, which was just what Sam needed after Ferguson's mention of The Drop Zone had conjured images of a Laurel's kiss-swollen lips and that damn sexy yellow dress.

With over a hundred pounds of gear strapped to each of their backs, their progress was slow going. Still, Sam welcomed the physical activity. Now that he had time to process the scene from the bar last night, his annoyance began to churn in his gut again. Even worse, none of his feelings made a lick of sense. He wanted his relationship with Laurel to be casual, no strings attached. But when she had told Straight Air Johnson that they weren't involved, something cold had seemed to seize Sam's insides.

Damn it. He slashed at a vine that blocked their path. Laurel wanted a man who could give her and her son a quiet, risk-free life—even if that life was contrary to her impetuous nature. As much as he wanted to be, Sam wasn't that man. His job involved risk and it was a career he excelled at. One he thrived on. He hadn't been able to give up his life for Becky and he wouldn't give it up for Laurel.

With a fierce hack, Sam leveled a branch with his pulaski. Laurel would never go for the just sex plan, either, no matter how intense the physical connection was between them. It didn't matter how loudly her body called to him, her declaration at The Drop Zone that they weren't a couple was even louder. She was living her life for her son, and the parts of Sam above his belt respected her for it.

Tyson needed a male role model who was a more constant part of his life than the selfish ass he already had for a father. Sam angrily pushed a small log with the heel of his boot, rolling it down the hill. He hated how Bryce Johnson was throwing away his opportunity at fatherhood. An opportunity Sam had lost before he even knew he'd had it. And it angered him further that Laurel was giving up on her dreams so she could be both mother and father to her son.

"Cap, I think it's already dead," Ferguson said from behind him.

Sam looked up from a bush he was pruning back to a twig to see three sets of anxious eyes trained on him. *Damn.* He needed to get his mind off Laurel Keenan and back onto his work. This was why he didn't do relationships. If he'd learned one thing from his failure of a marriage, it was that he couldn't have both.

"Why don't I take the point for a while?" Dodson stepped ahead of Sam. "If you keep that up for the next eight miles, you'll need a new rotator cuff."

Sam nodded, falling in behind Ferguson who proceeded to butcher several Keith Urban songs while they hiked. By the time they reached the pick-up point five-and-a-half hours later, Sam needed some ibuprofen, a hot shower, and a bed, in that order.

"The investigators from the NTSB are waiting back at the base," Miranda announced as Sam hoisted his pack into the back of the van. "They have some questions they need to ask you before they can file their report."

He groaned as he climbed into the passenger seat. Ferguson was thankfully sprawled on the far back seat, his snores already filling the van while Dodson and Rivers shared the middle bench seat.

"Perfect," Sam said. "Talking to bureaucrats is just what I want to do after spending the last twenty-four hours in the woods."

As it turned out, the investigators' questions were brief and to the point. Something Sam appreciated after the long hike and the hour car ride back to Glacier Creek. When he'd arrived back at the forest service station, only the on-call staff remained and they were engaged in a fierce game of HORSE at the basketball hoop. He stowed his gear in the ready room where it would be waiting for a thorough cleaning the next day. Then he went to his office to review the paperwork Jacqui had left on his desk, smiling to himself when he saw her sticky note that Pfeiffer had dropped out of rookie camp that afternoon.

The sun was low in the sky when Sam finally steered his truck up the drive leading to the A-frame, tucked high above Flathead Lake. His body was screaming for a beer and a soft pillow. Clearly, exhaustion was playing tricks on his brain because as he parked in front of the cabin he noticed a woman seated on the steps leading to the porch. A woman dressed for trouble in tight jeans, turquoise cowboy boots, and a straw cowboy hat. Sam swore as he killed the engine. He hesitated a moment before getting out of the driver's seat. Climbing the stairs, he kept his back to her as he unlocked the front door.

"What are you doing here, Laurel?"

CHAPTER NINE

L AUREL SHIFTED UNCOMFORTABLY on the wooden step. *This was such a bad idea.* But she'd wanted to see firsthand that Sam was okay. When Ivy offered to take Tyson with her nephews to the minor league baseball game, Laurel had jumped at the chance of a few hours to study. Instead she had camped out on Sam's front porch, waiting for him to return. Apparently, her impulsiveness was firmly back in the driver's seat.

"What are you doing here, Laurel?"

Not exactly the welcome she was hoping for, but after her abject denial that they were a couple in front of everyone at The Drop Zone, she should have expected Sam's miffed tone. What she hadn't anticipated were the agonizing emotions the sight of a filthy, bone-weary Sam churned up inside of her. Laurel felt the same helplessness and fear she experienced every time Tyson was sick. Which was ridiculous because Sam was a grown man capable of taking care of himself.

She stood up from the porch, brushing her hands down her jeans. "I wanted to make sure you were all right."

He turned to face her then, his eyes fierce in his tired face. "Of course, I'm all right, Laurel. I'm not some rookie making his first jump. I'm a professional. One of the best."

Laurel fought not to roll her eyes. "Why must guys always mistake genuine caring for an attack on their manhood?"

"I'm fine, Laurel," he practically growled. "You've done your good deed for the day. You can take the Little Red Riding Hood routine back to the ranch now."

Sam pushed open the front door and stepped inside. Laurel raced to follow him into the cabin before he could shut the door in her face.

"*Good deed?*" she sputtered. "*Little Red Riding Hood?* Did you get conked on the head while you were out fighting that fire?"

Sam sank down on a bench just inside the door and began pulling off his boots. "I must have because I don't remember inviting you in."

"I'm here because I care what happens to you! Because we're—we're . . ." She couldn't quite get her mouth to spit out the word *lovers*. It sounded so tawdry. Yet that was what they were to one another. Nothing more. And the thought made her sad. Suddenly, she wanted more with this man. She wanted Sam to be the guy she could spend her life with; to raise Tyson with. But he wasn't offering that. And she couldn't settle for less. She wouldn't.

Sam's expression was hard as he paused in the act of unlacing his boot. "We're what, Laurel?"

She wrapped her arms around her midsection. His ego had been dinged when she'd publically rejected him last night, she got that. But the depth of his anger confused her. "We're friends," she said softly.

The sound of his boot dropping to the floor echoed throughout the small cabin. He didn't say anything as he stood up and marched toward the kitchen at the back of the A-frame. Laurel followed behind him, surreptitiously taking in the starkness of the living area. Sam had lived in Glacier Creek for a month, yet he hadn't made any effort to make the cabin his own.

"I know you're mad about what I said last night," Laurel said as she entered the modern kitchen with its panoramic view of the Rocky Mountains. "But I honestly didn't know how to define our relationship when both of us can't even figure out what this is between us."

He was mute as he pulled a beer from the fridge and opened the tab. Reaching into a cabinet, Sam took out a bottle of ibuprofen. He downed three of the tablets with a healthy swallow of beer. Laurel opened her mouth to point out that mixing medicine with alcohol probably wasn't a good idea, but when she met Sam's annoyed gaze, she thought better of it.

"You just defined what 'this' is, Laurel," he said as he slid past her, making his way up the stairs to the bedroom. "We're friends. You just conveniently ignored the *with benefits* aspect of our friendship."

"If that's the case, then why are you so angry?" she demanded as she stomped up the stairs after him.

"Jesus, woman, I'm not angry. I'm fucking tired. And filthy." He yanked off his Henley and his T-shirt and tossed them into a pile on the floor. "The last thing I want to do tonight is stand around here and talk about my feelings. Instead, what I want is a hot shower and a soft bed. You're welcome to join me in either or both of those, but not if you're going to examine our relationship under a microscope the whole time."

Sam yanked at his zipper and shoved his jeans and his black boxer briefs down his muscled legs. Laurel swallowed roughly, watching him stroll naked toward the large walk-in shower. He chugged what remained of his beer while the water heated up, never bothering to spare a glance at her.

Bull crap, he wasn't angry. She should call him out on it, but she didn't want to be a bully after he'd spent the last twenty-four hours fighting a fire. Instead, she stood motionless, foolishly admiring the view.

Get out, her heart and her brain yelled at her. But her feet seemed to be glued to the floor. Sam stepped into the shower and Laurel tossed her hat onto the bed in defeat. *Just once more,* she reasoned with herself. *It's likely to be another long dry spell after this.*

Laurel toed off her boots and stripped before she could change her mind. If Sam was surprised when she slipped into the two-person shower, he didn't show it. His only tell was a slight softening of his mouth as he massaged shampoo into his scalp.

Water from the three jets sluiced over his hard body and Laurel cataloged the cuts, scrapes, and bruises that hadn't been there a day ago. *Battle scars from his profession.* She ignored the anxiety his wounds provoked, instead pouring body wash into her palm before stepping behind Sam. He groaned softly when she began to knead the muscles on his shoulders before trailing her fingers down his spine. She inhaled the scent of soap and aroused male as her lips followed her fingers over his slick skin. White heat shot to her core the more she touched him. Unable to contain herself any longer, Laurel reached her hands around Sam's torso to wrap her fingers around his erection. He swore when she pressed her wet body flat against his, her teeth grazing his shoulder.

Swiftly, Sam spun around and dipped his head to kiss her. His mouth was demanding and the force of their kiss had her leaning on the smooth tile of the shower for support. The soapy suds created an exciting friction between their bodies and Laurel wrapped her hands around Sam's neck to keep from sliding to the floor. He reached for her leg and lifted her knee so her calf wrapped around his ass. Taking her mouth in another hungry kiss, he slipped a finger inside of her, teasing her sweet spot.

"Sam," she cried. "Please."

He entered her with one single thrust and the pleasure was so exquisite Laurel banged her head against the wall. Sam shifted their bodies so the spray of the water was at his back as he pushed into her again and again.

Sam abruptly stilled, causing a moan of frustration to escape Laurel's chest.

"Open your eyes, Laurel," he demanded.

Her breathing was fractured and she could only manage to lift her eyelids halfway. Sam's gaze was intense as he studied her, his eyes seeming to encourage her when he slid in sharply again and again. Her climax overtook her without warning, the intensity of it nearly forcing her to her knees had she not had her arms locked around Sam's shoulders.

Sam's mouth grew tight as her body convulsed around him. He swore and jerked free of her. Using his elbow, he pressed the lever controlling the water so that the jets turned off. Then he pushed open the shower door. He grabbed for a bath sheet and wrapped it around Laurel's trembling body before guiding her toward the bedroom.

She sat on the edge of the bed as Sam dug through the pile of clothes to retrieve his wallet. Laurel would have laughed at his desperation, but the pained look on his face stopped her. The hunger and heat in his eyes took her breath away. She leaned back on her elbows, letting the towel fall open in invitation. He hissed when he rolled the condom over his erection.

"Flip," he commanded as he prowled toward the bed.

Laurel sucked in a breath before doing as he asked. His body was damp and hot when it covered hers. Reaching beneath her stomach he lifted her up to her hands and knees. Sam's breath was raspy against her ear. His fingers found her nipples. She rocked back against his arousal and he took her earlobe between his teeth. The pleasure and the pain of it made her cry out.

Sam reached for her hip with one of his hands, anchoring her body to his as he slid inside of her. "This is what our relationship is, Laurel," he said. "This amazing physical connection."

He began to move inside of her, slowly at first, making her body anxious and fretful. She writhed beneath him, but he didn't adjust the pace. His finger slipped down between her legs to flick over her sweet spot, teasing her body so it was drawn tight like a bow. Laurel squirmed even more, desperate to find her release.

"Damn it, Sam!" He'd reduced to her begging again.

"This is all I can give you, Laurel." He breathed the words next to her ear. "I wish I could give you more, but I can't. I'd only fuck it up. And you deserve more. You deserve a guy who can give you his whole heart."

He drove in and out of her then, his powerful thrusts shaking the bed. Laurel was glad to have her back to him, so he wouldn't see the tears his words had brought to her eyes. She didn't want another guy's heart. She wanted Sam's.

Her climax was the catalyst to his. Sam sank his teeth

into her shoulder when his body shook with his release. They stayed upright for several long moments, Sam's body cocooning hers while their breathing slowly returned to normal.

"I can't do this anymore." Laurel was glad she was able to get the words out without her voice breaking.

"I know." Sam sighed as he brushed his lips over the spot where he'd bit her. "I wish I could be the guy you deserve, Laurel."

Somehow Laurel thought Sam *could* be that guy—even with the whole jumping out of airplanes part of his life. But he had closed off his heart when his wife had died. Laurel had already been refused a man's love once, although this time stung a lot more than Bryce's rejection had. But she always had Tyson. Once again, her son's unconditional love would have to be enough.

Sam fell back onto the mattress, exhaustion already claiming his body. Laurel slipped from the bed, spreading a blanket over Sam before gathering up her clothes.

"Laurel." His voice was raspy with sleep as he called out to her. "Stop trying to deny who you are. Tyson could do a lot worse than having a mother who's a starving artist. Bryce shouldn't be the only one allowed to go after his dreams."

She hurried down the stairs so that Sam wouldn't hear her sobs.

SAM SET THE stopwatch on his phone and glanced up at the rookie suspended from the jump tower. "You have two minutes to get your ass out of that tree, McCoy," he shouted. "Starting *now!*"

McCoy quickly checked to make sure his parachute was securely hung up on the jump tower that was doubling as a 'tree' before determining all of its suspension lines were clear of his body. He then released his reserve parachute and his PG pack. Reaching into the right pant leg of his jump suit, he pulled out a carabiner and two friction rings that were sewn into the pocket. Then he pulled out about eight feet of the letdown tape that was housed in the pants, quickly and efficiently threading the tape through the rings and wrapping it around his body twice. With a one-armed pull up, McCoy pulled the tape taut and tied it off with a slip-knot. Keeping the slack tight, he untied the letdown tape from his pocket and let it drop to the ground. He shifted his weight from the harness to the letdown tape and began the slow, smooth descent to the ground. The crew of smokejumpers that were watching McCoy's progress applauded when he landed safely.

"A minute fifty," Sam called out. "Excellent, McCoy." He turned to address the rest of the rookies, now down to ten at the beginning of week two. "It's imperative that you all master the letdown procedure. A limb landing is a big deal because it holds up the rest of the team. The spotter can't drop the cargo until he or she knows everyone is on the ground. These are minutes that matter when it comes to fire fighting. The whole operation has to stop until they get your ass out of that tree. Only three of you managed to get down in under two minutes. The rest of you had better spend tonight working on that letdown procedure or you won't be making your training jump tomorrow."

The rookies groaned while the veterans laughed. A few of the old-timers offered to help out the rookies in exchange for having their trucks washed. Sam left them to it and headed inside to his office. The ten remaining rookies would finally be jumping from an actual airplane tomorrow. While there wouldn't be any danger they'd get hung up on a tree—they'd be landing in pasture—things could still go wrong. Each of them would have a radio in their pocket with an experienced smokejumper calling out guidance during their jump, but Sam believed in preparing for every contingency.

The fire season was fast approaching and he was anxious that he be fully prepared for what awaited him. Throwing himself into his work also meant he spent less time at his cabin. Sam hadn't realized how lonely he was in the A-frame until he'd woken up the morning after Laurel had been there. His pillow still bore her scent a week later. Every time he got in the shower, he saw her there against the tile, flushed and eager to give herself to him.

Sam wasn't accustomed to craving a woman the way his body wanted Laurel's. Even worse, he missed her. He missed her quick wit, her cocky smile, and her impulsive nature.

She'd gotten under his skin and he wasn't sure how to get her out. So he buried himself in work.

"Sam," Jacqui called as he passed the reception desk, "you have a message here from Wayne Keenan."

He strolled back over to the front of the two-story lobby. From where she sat, Jacqui had a bird's eye view of her late husband's parachute. Sam wasn't sure if the sight of it brought her great pain or peace, but regardless, Jacqui was always on task. Her presence at the base had brought a little calm and order these past two weeks and Sam was appreciative of her professionalism.

"Did he say what he wanted?" Sam asked.

Jacqui exchanged a look with Miranda Ferguson. The pilot had the next day's jump schedule spread out on the reception desk.

"He just asked if you could stop by the ranch this evening," Jacqui replied.

Sam swallowed a groan. He'd purposely been avoiding Whispering Breeze this past week so as not to run into Laurel. Seeing her without being able to touch her would be too much torture. And he wanted to do the gentlemanly thing by honoring her decision—no matter how much it killed him. But if something was wrong with Tabitha, Sam needed to check it out. He swore under his breath.

"Hey, Jacqui, do you want to grab some dinner?" Miranda was saying. "Laurel is off in Kalispell tonight at a study seminar, but Ivy and I are going to check out the new Thai restaurant."

Miranda was looking at Sam as she spoke, not being shy about the message she was telegraphing. Jacqui bit back a smile as she glanced between the pilot and Sam. "Um, yeah, that sounds fun."

They gazed at him expectantly. Sam blew out a resigned sigh. He was being handled by these two women who likely knew all about his and Laurel's brief fling. Being women, they probably had some sort of romantic notion that things would work out between them.

They'd be wrong.

"You sure you didn't have a career in covert ops?" he asked Miranda.

She laughed. "I have four brothers, captain."

"Mmm." Sam nodded. "I'll head over to the ranch after I check those jump schedules for tomorrow." He took the schedules from Miranda and headed back to his office, knowing both women were smiling smugly as he walked away.

An hour later, Sam pulled up the long drive toward the ranch. He parked his truck in the roundabout. Sam was relieved that Laurel's Land Cruiser was nowhere in sight. Cheech and Chong, the two alpacas, were standing in their pen humming loudly, presumably calling for their dinner. Truman the goat trotted out of the barn to greet Sam, but he was quickly distracted by a bale of hay.

Sam decided to check on Tabitha before seeking out

Keenan. He strolled into the barn, pulling up short when he saw a woman in a wheelchair outside of the wash stall. Precocious green eyes, so like her daughter's, met his. She was holding the lead rope with Tabitha attached to the other end. The mare was standing patiently while Wayne Keenan held her hoof in a bucket of water. Smiling kindly, Laurel's mother gestured for him to come closer.

"I'm so glad you're here, captain," she said. "I've been wondering when I'd finally meet you."

Sam approached cautiously. Jo Keenan was wearing the identical smug look Miranda had been sporting an hour ago, as if she knew all and she was determined for a different outcome.

"What happened to her?" he asked.

Wayne Keenan looked up from his crouched position next to Tabitha. "Abscess. Laurel felt it as soon as she got on her today. The girl is like the princess and the pea. She can detect even the slightest change in a horse's gait days before it goes lame. The farrier has been by and she took off the shoe. We caught it early, so she'll only need a few days of soaking and this girl will be right as rain by the weekend." He patted Tabitha's withers.

Sam stroked a finger done the horse's nose. "That's good. Whatever she needs to heal, I'm happy to foot the bill."

"She just needs a little TLC, that's all," Jo Keenan said. Tabitha dipped her head into the woman's lap. Jo planted a kiss on the horse's nose.

Relief warred with a bit of envy as Sam took in the scene before him. Becky's horse had moved on, transferring its devotion to another. He was glad for the bond between both the animal and the disabled woman. Yet something inside of him wanted to rail that Tabitha would always be Becky's horse.

"She'll have to heal fast. I have some potential buyers headed up from California this weekend."

Keenan's words were like a sucker punch to Sam's gut. "You have buyers interested already?"

"I posted some videos this weekend of Laurel working her through some drills. She made the mare look amazing," Keenan said proudly.

Sam swallowed roughly. He'd always known he'd sell the horse. He just wasn't prepared for the tumult of emotions that would come along with Tabitha leaving. She was his last connection to Becky. Even more troubling, the mare was his link to Laurel Keenan. Once Tabitha was gone, he'd have no excuse to visit the ranch.

"Of course..." Jo Keenan interrupted his thoughts. "If you're not eager to sell yet, Tabitha could always stay here and Laurel and I could take her to the Quarter Horse Congress in the fall. Not to brag or anything, but my daughter is your best chance of winning." The woman eyed him shrewdly. "The horse will be worth more then. Unless you need the money a sale would bring now."

Sam bristled. "This has never been about the money. It's

been about honoring my late wife's wishes."

"Which was for Tabitha to ride at the national level?"

He nodded brusquely.

Jo Keenan gave him a coy look as she patted Tabitha's nose. "It's settled then. Tabitha will stay here at Whispering Breeze and Laurel will take her to the championship."

Wayne Keenan opened his mouth to say something, but his wife silenced him with a look. He shot Sam a resigned glance. "If that's what everyone wants."

Sam wasn't sure what had just happened. The smart thing to do would be to sell the horse and get rid of the temptation Laurel Keenan presented. But Sam clearly wasn't thinking with his brain right now. His relief at still having a connection with Laurel was palpable.

"What if she doesn't want to do it?" he asked.

Laurel's mother smiled knowingly. "You leave her to me, captain."

With a roll of his eyes, Wayne Keenan led the horse back to its stall.

"Will you stay for supper, captain? It's just the three of us tonight, but I made a pot roast." Jo Keenan looked at him expectantly.

The only thing in Sam's refrigerator was a frozen pizza. His stomach rumbled embarrassingly at the mention of food.

Wayne Keenan slapped him on the shoulder as he passed by. "It's no use arguing with her, son. And you won't get a better meal anywhere in Glacier Creek."

Supper with the Keenans and Tyson was more relaxing than Sam expected. Months of eating alone or among strangers at a restaurant had made him forget the joy of a simple family dinner. Growing up, his father had always insisted on their family dining together when he was in country. Even the camaraderie of eating with his platoon had been pleasant for Sam. He hadn't realized how much he missed it until this evening.

"Tyson, we'd best get you into the tub soon," Jo Keenan said after her grandson had devoured a bowl of ice cream showered in rainbow sprinkles. The boy had been subdued during most of the meal. Sam figured he likely missed his mother. "I promised your mama you'd be in bed before nine."

Sam carried his glass and plate into the kitchen. The state-of-the-art room had been reconfigured with low counters and wheelchair accessible appliances so Jo Keenan could still indulge in her love of cooking. Based on the delicious dinner Sam had just savored, he had no doubt of the reason her husband had spared no expense.

"Captain, you just leave those," she called from the dining room. "Wayne is in charge of cleaning up."

Wayne Keenan smiled fondly at his wife. "It's the price I pay for her fine cooking."

"Thank you, ma'am. Dinner was delicious. I'm just going to check in on Tabitha on my way out." Sam waved to Laurel's father and headed out the door toward the barn.

Cheech and Chong were still humming softly when Sam made his way into the barn. The one-eyed cat snaked its way between Sam's legs as he walked to Tabitha's stall. The mare eyed him stoically while keeping her distance.

"That abscess doesn't seem to be bothering you too much," Sam said to the horse.

"She's gonna be fine, aren't you, girl." Tyson scrambled up onto a step stool. He placed his arms on the stall door, mirroring Sam's exact pose. "I'm gonna be a veterinarian when I grow up. Did you know that?"

Sam couldn't help but smile at the boy's determined posture. "Either that or an escape artist. Aren't you supposed to be in the bathtub?"

"In a minute. I need to say goodnight to the animals first."

They stood there quietly for a few moments, listening as the barn settled around them. Even the alpacas' humming had quieted.

"I'm glad Tabitha's staying." Tyson's voice wavered. "Mama would be more sad if she left. She's been crying a lot this week. She thinks I don't hear her, but I do."

Guilt twisted Sam's insides into a knot. He should never have pursued her. But her pull had been too strong for his body to ignore. Hurting her had never been part of his plan.

"It's because Daddy won't come live here after the 'lympics."

Sam glanced over at the boy.

Tyson's lip quivered slightly as he spoke. "It's 'cause of me."

"Whoa, there, sport." Instinctively, Sam reached over and placed his hand in the middle of the boy's back. He was instantly reminded this child of a daredevil and an impetuous woman was just that, a child, in spite of his worldly mannerisms. The bones and muscles beneath Sam's palm were still slight and in need of nurturing.

"Just because your dad doesn't live here with you and your mom doesn't mean he doesn't love you both." It stuck in Sam's craw that he had to defend that egotistical jerk, Bryce Johnson. But he knew Laurel wouldn't want her son thinking such troublesome thoughts. "Lots of families are that way."

"That's what Mama says." Tyson wouldn't meet Sam's eyes. "But the big kids at school say it's because my mom had to come back here to take care of me."

Sam swore beneath his breath, cursing out every tabloid and gossip show for convoluting the facts. None of those parasites ever thought of the impact those tall tales had on the innocent children.

He put his hands on Tyson's scrawny shoulders and spun him around so that they were eye to eye. "Don't listen to those bullies, Tyson. Your mom came back because she knew how much you were going to love animals and she wanted you to grow up on a ranch. That's how much she loves you."

Tyson's eyes were shining, but a corner of his lip wriggled up. "She's a great mommy," he said softly. He suddenly jerked out of Sam's grasp. "Wait here," he called before scurrying up the stairs to the loft.

He returned a minute later carrying a large piece of thick paper. When Tyson turned it for Sam to see, his breath caught in his lungs. It was a charcoal rendering of Tabitha, the mare's eyes looking so lifelike it was as if she was staring back from the paper.

"Mama draw'd it for you. So you'd be able to 'member Tabitha when she goes to live at another barn. It's good, huh?"

It was better than good. It was spectacular. "Yeah, your mom is very talented."

Tyson's lip began to tremble again. "Daddy said she was gonna be an artist but she changed her mind when she had me."

Bryce Johnson was lucky he was a continent away because Sam was ready to tear him apart with his bare hands.

"Tyson!" Jo Keenan called from the house. "Your bath is almost ready."

Tyson shoved the drawing into Sam's hands. "Even though Tabitha is staying, you should keep this. Mama was gonna give it to you anyway. See you later, captain!" He scooted off before Sam could return the drawing.

CHAPTER TEN

"**D**OES UNCLE LIAM jump from that big tower?"

Tyson had his faced pressed to the window, peering out at the smokejumpers going through their afternoon PT workout on the field in front of the forest service station. Laurel pulled her Land Cruiser into the gravel lot and parked next to Miranda's Sebring convertible.

"I'm sure he does," Laurel responded absently. She scoured the crowded lawn, looking for Sam.

Tyson unbuckled his booster seatbelt and scrambled down to the floor. "I'll bet the captain jumps faster and better than Uncle Liam."

Laurel's stomach clenched at the thought of Sam jumping out of an airplane, hurtling his body into a fire. Funny, she'd known Liam longer, and she didn't have the same agonizing nausea when she thought of him doing the same thing. Probably because smokejumping was a part of Liam and Uncle Hugh's DNA, just as their laughing blue eyes were. It was a part of them that Laurel saw, but was immune to.

She opened the back door and Tyson jumped down.

"Can I go find Uncle Liam?"

"We'll only be here a minute. I just need to find the captain and have a quick word with him." She took Tyson by the hand and marched over to the big field.

Her mother's announcement that Laurel would be riding Tabitha at the Quarter Horse Congress later this year had been as unexpected as the positive pregnancy test six years ago. And nearly as devastating. Having Tabitha at the ranch meant Sam still had an excuse to pop into her real life just as he did her dreams every night. It was just too much. He'd been understanding about her reasons for not continuing their relationship. His agreement that Laurel should ride Tabitha made no sense.

"There he is!" Tyson pointed to one side of the field where groups of men were flipping a giant tractor tire from one end to the other. "Wow! The captain is stronger than X-Man."

The excited reverence in Tyson's voice was nothing compared to the dance Laurel's ovaries were doing at the sight of Sam, shirtless with muscles rippling. The crew of smokejumpers cheered as he flipped his tire across the finish line before two of the other men. Tyson whooped along with the rest of them, his exuberant voice catching Sam's attention.

Sam's face went from surprised to tense as his gaze wandered from Tyson to Laurel. He picked up his T-shirt from the grass and wiped his hands and face with it as he wandered through the crowd toward them.

"How heavy are those tires?" Tyson asked as he wriggled from Laurel's grasp. "They look ginormous!"

"Why don't you go check them out?" Sam gestured toward the tire.

Tyson dashed off before Laurel could snatch him back.

"Relax, those things aren't going anywhere," Sam said when Laurel took a step to chase after her son. "McCoy, can you keep an eye on Tyson for a minute?"

Dex McCoy strolled by Laurel and gave her a wink. "Sure thing, Cap."

"When did you start jumping, Dex?" Laurel was astonished to see her neighbor at the base. Dex was a rancher through and through. He'd always intended to take over his father's ranch. She'd heard rumors about some sort of rift with Dex's older brother, but she was surprised at his sudden career change.

"Jumped for the first time today," he said. Excitement was shining in his eyes as he fist-bumped with Sam. "It was awesome."

Laurel shook her head. "You're all crazy," she mumbled.

Sam crossed his arms over his chest. "What brings you out among the crazies then, Laurel?"

"We need to talk."

A muscle twitched at the corner of his mouth. "Fine. Let's go inside."

Laurel glanced over at Tyson, who was trying with all his

might to lift the tractor tire.

Sam sighed. "You don't need a human shield to talk with me, Laurel. We can go to my office."

She hated the way he saw right through her. "No," she said shaking her head.

"Don't you trust me to keep my hands to myself?"

"It's not you I'm worried about," she said begrudgingly.

Sam grinned. His devastating dimple made her stomach do a somersault. "God, I've missed you and your honesty."

His admission made her throat thick.

"So what are we going to talk about?"

"Tabitha."

His smile froze. "I thought the abscess wasn't serious?"

Laurel waved a hand in the air. "It isn't. She's already walking better on it. It's not that. It's the crazy plan of my mother's. Why on earth did you agree to it?"

"Have you met your mother?" Sam chuckled. "She's a pretty formidable woman. I can't imagine what she was like before the wheelchair."

She nearly laughed. "Trust me, that wheelchair has become my mom's secret weapon." Laurel suddenly remembered that she was angry with him. "Did you ever consider asking me what I wanted?"

His dimple was long gone. "I wasn't exactly given the chance. You're more than welcome to tell your mother no."

He was calling her bluff. Sam knew she couldn't tell her mother no any more than he could.

Sam dropped his defensive posture and brought a hand up to squeeze the back of his neck. "Look, if you really don't want to do it, I'll sell her."

"No!" Laurel wrapped her arms around herself. She hated that she was being an indecisive ninny. She wanted the horse to go, but the thought of Tabitha leaving was as painful as never seeing Sam again. "Never mind. My mom is getting too much out of it to end this whole thing now. I'll manage the extra work. I just—I just…"

Laurel got lost in his perceptive amber eyes.

"It's just that you don't want me around," he said softly. "I get it. I'll be gone all summer. You won't have to worry about seeing me. When I'm in town, I'll be busy with the base."

Her throat grew even tighter and her eyes stung just thinking about Sam constantly putting himself in harm's way.

"Mommy! Look at me!"

Laurel stared over at Tyson. He was lifting the tire with the help of Dex McCoy and Liam on either side of him. "I'm almost as strong as the captain."

Tyler Dodson laughed. "You keep practicing, Champ, and you might be able to beat him in pull-ups someday."

The rest of the crew joined in the laughter.

"I should go," Laurel said. "We're distracting you all from your work."

Before she could take a step, Sam reached out and

grasped her arm. She looked down at his fingers wrapped around her skin. Sweet warmth pooled in her belly at the contact.

"Before you go, I have something to tell you about Tyson."

Looking back up at him, she shrugged off his hand. "What about him?" Something in Sam's gaze told her she wasn't going to like what she was going to hear.

Sam hesitated, making Laurel more anxious. "Last night he told me that you'd been crying all week." He looked away for a moment. She watched the muscles in his neck contract as he swallowed roughly. "I'm sorry that I hurt you."

A hundred denials rose to her lips but she couldn't seem to form any of them into words.

His eyes seemed to understand what she couldn't say and he nodded. "You need to know that Tyson thinks you're upset because Bryce isn't coming to live with you after the Olympics." He sighed irritably. "Tyson thinks it's his fault somehow."

She regretted shaking his hand away because it was a struggle for Laurel to stay upright. Forcing a few deep breaths in and out of her lungs, she looked over at her son who was laughing while Dex and Liam tossed him back and forth.

"I've tried explaining this all to him."

"He's young. He'll be more accepting of things as he matures," Sam said. His words weren't as reassuring as he had likely intended.

Laurel nodded jerkily. "I have to go."

"Laurel, wait." Sam fell into step beside her. "Please know that I'm here if you ever need something. Anything."

She stopped in her tracks. Her eyes burned with unshed tears but she managed to get the words out anyway. "The one thing I need, you can't give me."

THE JUNE SKY was growing dark when Sam slipped into Cady's Cakes for a coffee and a donut. He'd been on the phone with the tactical coordinator most of the day, assessing manpower in anticipation of the storm moving into the area. So far this spring, most of the fires his crews had handled were the result of accidents or human error. The threat of lightning, however, could be a game changer, and Sam needed to be prepared.

"Hey there, Cap," Molly Rivers called from one of the small bistro tables where she sat with an older woman. "Glad to see you actually eating something. Liam's been telling everyone around the base that you're secretly a robot."

"Molly." The older woman chastised her. "Is that any way to talk to your boss?"

Rivers laughed. "Mom, the man has been working eighteen-hour days, seven days a week for the past month. He's putting the rest of us to shame with his superhero work ethic."

Sam stood at the counter and stirred some creamer into his coffee. Burying himself in his job had always been his catharsis. Work was the one thing in life he was successful at, and he wasn't going to apologize to Molly Rivers or anyone else for his work ethic. "Just doing what they pay me to do."

Molly and her mother rose from their table. Mrs. Rivers carried their trash to the can at the other end of the counter while Molly came to stand beside Sam.

"You're a phenomenal leader, captain," she said quietly. "I can't imagine anyone else I'd want managing our crews. Take my word for it; everyone at the base feels the same way. But you'll be no good to any of us if you burn yourself out the first month of the fire season."

It wasn't Sam's intention to burn himself out. His only goal was to work so hard that when he fell into bed at night he was too exhausted to dream about Laurel Keenan and her bewitching body. It had been four weeks since she'd turned her back on him at Dead Man's Valley. She'd cut him to the quick with her words. Laurel had practically admitted she loved him, and Sam was still reeling from the aftershocks. He'd risk his body every day, but his heart was a different story. Sam had been down that road before only to fail miserably.

"I'm glad I didn't see her in here before I had that cheesecake," Molly's mother was saying. "There's no better appetite suppressant than the sight of a gorgeous supermodel."

Sam followed her gaze across the room to where Tyson sat on a chair, picking at a cupcake. Bryce Johnson sat across from him holding hands with a beautiful woman Sam recognized from the *Sports Illustrated* swimsuit edition.

"The least she could do is nibble on a cookie or something," Molly said. "Damn. Now I'm going to have to head back to base and work off my scone. See you back there, Cap."

The two women headed out of the bakery. Sam should have followed them, but something about the way Tyson's lip was quivering forced his feet in a different direction.

"Hey there, Sport," Sam said when he'd reached their table. His hand twitched to reassure the boy with a pat on the back. One look at Bryce Johnson's stony face and Sam resisted the temptation.

Tyson's face lit up with a hopeful look when he spied Sam before his eyes dimmed again quickly. "Hi, captain."

"How's Tabitha doing?" Sam asked. "I hope you're taking good care of her for me."

"Yes, sir." The boy nodded.

"Tyson was just telling us how strong you are, captain." Bryce leaned back in his chair, a challenging grin on his face. "I'm always looking for ways to improve my workout. Perhaps one day you and I could train together. You know, soldier takes on Olympian. It would be interesting to see which one has more stamina. The media would eat it up."

Sam wanted to tell the guy Molly Rivers likely had more

stamina than Johnson did, but he kept his opinion to himself. He wasn't sure if Johnson was posturing for his son or his fiancée. Either way, Sam wasn't going to get pulled into a battle of testosterone with the jock.

"We're in the middle of fire season right now. There's not much time for showing off."

Johnson flinched slightly. "Well, if you're not up to it." He shrugged.

It was all Sam could do not to wipe the smug grin off Johnson's face. "Tyson, you give Tabitha a big hug for me, okay?" He reached over and gave the boy's shoulder a gentle squeeze, ignoring Johnson's narrowed eyes when he did so. "I know she's in good hands with you watching over her."

With a nod at Johnson and the silent work of art sitting next to him, Sam headed for the door.

"Captain!"

Tyson jumped from his chair and raced over to Sam. Crouching down, Sam glanced into the boy's moist eyes.

"He's marrying *her*," Tyson whispered.

Sam looked past the boy, but Johnson and his fiancée seemed to be engrossed in a heated conversation.

"That doesn't mean he loves you any less." Sam tried to reassure Tyson. "Now you'll just have someone else to love you, too." As platitudes went, it was pretty lame, but Sam didn't want the child to feel abandoned.

Tyson's lip quivered again. "But what if I have to go live with them? I don't want to leave the ranch. Or Miss Ivy. Or

Grandpa and Grandma. Or Mama."

Sam doubted Bryce Johnson would make room for his son now that he had a wife, but he couldn't be completely sure. Tyson's fear was understandable. He hesitated, not knowing what to say to calm the boy's anxiety.

Johnson's hand landed on the boy's shoulder. "Hey, Halfpipe, you promised to show Audrianna the animal sanctuary. It's looking like rain out there, so we'd better get a move on." He handed the boy an ugly stuffed frog.

Tyson's chin dropped to his chest and Sam's chest squeezed tightly.

"Bye, captain." Tyson shuffled out of the bakery, the frog hanging loosely from his fingertips.

Sam stood up, watching them go. He debated with himself whether or not he should tell Laurel about Tyson's fears. Except the last time he'd gotten involved, he'd only ended up saying something that hurt her.

The radio beeped in Sam's pocket. He was needed back at the base. Tyson had nothing to worry about, Sam told himself. Laurel would never give up her son willingly. She'd already sacrificed so much of her life for him. Marginally reassured, he headed back to the forest service station where he could continue to drown himself in work.

IVY POPPED THE cork off the bottle and the champagne fizzled over the rim.

"Hey, don't waste that," Miranda said. She passed three champagne flutes over to Ivy.

"It's not like you can have any." Ivy poured a generous serving into two of the glasses. "You're on call, remember?"

"With this storm rolling in, we're all pretty much grounded for the next twelve hours," Miranda argued. "I can have a sip so that we can toast Laurel's surviving the exam."

Laurel glanced around the crowded Drop Zone. Despite the impending storm, it seemed that half the population of Glacier Creek had crammed into the bar. While most of the crew from the forest service station was milling about, she was relieved to not see Sam among them. It had been four weeks since she'd left him standing in Dead Man's Valley. The look of devastation she'd thought she'd glimpsed in his eyes had surely been imagined because he'd kept his distance as promised. Yet that look still haunted her dreams at night. She couldn't understand why Sam wouldn't let himself love her.

"Earth to Laurel," Miranda said. She waved a champagne flute in front of Laurel. "We're toasting you here."

Pasting a smile on her face, she picked up her glass. "Sorry. My brain is still a little fried from all the studying."

"Well, I'm proud of you." Ivy held her glass up high. "You've established yourself in a career that will allow you to live comfortably."

"Yeah, one nobody saw coming," Miranda teased. "Here's to you, my favorite cousin."

"Isn't she your only cousin?" Ivy asked as they clinked glasses.

Laurel studied the amber liquid in her flute. "Yeah, well, at least everyone in this town can finally take me seriously. I'll be an independent woman and I won't have to live off the largess of my baby daddy any longer."

Ivy's eyes grew wide. "You might want to guzzle that, Laurel. Your baby daddy just walked in."

The murmurs that heralded Bryce and Audrianna's arrival reached a crescendo behind Laurel's back. She placed her champagne flute on the table untouched.

"Hello there, ladies," Bryce said as he stopped at their table. Audrianna hung back, posing for selfies with several of the patrons. "What are we celebrating?"

Miranda looked at him quizzically. "Laurel took the final part of the CPA exam today."

"I know that. I had to keep Tyson busy all day, remember?"

Laurel winced while Ivy downed her entire glass of champagne in one swallow. "I'm sorry for the inconvenience," Laurel said.

"Jesus, Laurel, can't you take a joke. It wasn't an 'inconvenience'. Although I think Tyson saw spending the day with Audrianna and me as one."

"Please tell me you told him about your wedding?"

"Yeah, that was our first mistake. We told him right away. It was all downhill after that."

Laurel sighed wearily. "He'll come around to the idea. He's still young."

"So you keep saying. Look, I suggested that maybe he come stay with us for a few weeks this summer and he nearly had a meltdown. Audrianna is beginning to take things personally."

She stood so abruptly her head began to spin. "Can we take things slow before you begin some great custody battle, Bryce?"

Bryce rocked back on his heels. "Is that what you think this is about? Look, Laurel, Tyson's more yours than he is mine. He always will be. That doesn't mean I don't love him or want to be a part of his life." He glanced over to where his fiancée was striking a pose with Liam as cellphone camera flashes went off. "Our lifestyle isn't really conducive to kids, you know?"

Laurel nodded, her stomach still in knots. "I'll do what I can to smooth things over."

"Maybe you should ask Soldier Sam, to help," Bryce said. "Tyson seems to worship the guy."

Laurel's head snapped up to meet Bryce's discerning stare. "I've got it handled. I don't need anyone's help."

"You never have." Bryce sighed. "Our plane has been grounded due to the weather. Your mom suggested we stay at the ranch so we could spend some time with Tyson in the morning. But if it's going to make you uncomfortable, we'll head up to Kalispell."

"It's fine," she said, despite the fact she felt anything but fine. "It'll give us a chance to promote a united front to him in the morning." Laurel grabbed her purse off the chair. "I should get home and get him ready for bed. You and Audrianna should finish the champagne."

Bryce reached for the bottle. "Don't mind if we do."

Ivy rolled her eyes. "I'll drive you home. This place is getting too crowded anyway."

CHAPTER ELEVEN

LAUREL SLEPT POORLY that night. The violent rain and hail had pounded the roof of the loft until well after midnight. She'd invited Tyson to come cuddle in bed with her, but he insisted that he was a big boy who wasn't afraid of storms. Too bad he refused to be reasonable about his father's wedding.

When Laurel had broached the subject during bedtime, Tyson had refused to discuss it. He insisted he had a plan and things would work out. Laurel had reassured him he would always live on the ranch with her. Her words seem to ease some of Tyson's stress. He'd given her a long hug before slipping under the covers. "You're the best mama ever," he'd told her. But his eyes had still been sad and Laurel remained unsettled for much of the evening.

A pounding on her door woke her just after seven-thirty. Bryce was apparently in a hurry to get out of town. "I'm coming," she said, dragging her tired body to the door.

But it wasn't Bryce on the other side. It was her father, looking grim. She heard the sound of horses pacing in their stalls below. "What is it? Is Mom okay?"

"Fire. In the west pasture. Lightning must have hit something out there last night. Help is on the way, but I need to get the horses loaded up."

Laurel had slipped her feet into her boots and pulled a sweatshirt from its hook before her father finished his succinct explanation. She clattered down the stairs toward the barn. The two stable hands were already placing halters on the horses and leading them out to the hauler. They'd wait in the horse trailer just in case Laurel had to quickly drive them to safety.

She dashed into Tabitha's stall and quickly placed a halter over the mare's head. Tabitha was skittish, aware of the danger animals seemed to innately sense. "Shh, baby." Laurel tried to sooth her. "You're gonna be okay. I'm not going to let anything happen to you." There wasn't time to wrap the horse's legs, so Laurel clipped on the lead rope and led the horse to the truck.

Bryce met her at the entrance of the barn. "What can I do to help?"

Laurel nearly kissed him. Bryce didn't have much expertise around animals, but here he was offering to pitch in a crisis. Deep down, she could count on him to be there for her and Tyson. "You can take Audrianna, my mom, and Tyson into town. Things are likely to get crazy here and if we have to leave in a hurry—" She swallowed painfully. The thought of losing the ranch made her chest ache. As much as she'd always wanted to get away, Whispering Breeze was her home. The place she wanted to raise her son.

Bryce hugged her. "It won't get to that." The sound of sirens racing up the drive refocused their attention. "You go get Tyson and I'll get your mother."

Laurel raced back up the stairs surprised her son hadn't already made his way down. The chaos below was creating a lot of noise, not to mention the arrival of the sirens. At the very least, Oreo should already be yipping. She slid the door open to her son's room and her breath seized in her lungs. His bed was empty. There was no sign of Tyson or his dog anywhere. Had he slipped downstairs while they were loading the horses?

She turned to grab his boots and his jacket, but both were missing. Laurel tried to call to her father or Bryce, but just like in those horrible dreams, she couldn't seem to make her voice work. On legs that were soft as noodles, she stumbled down the stairs to the barn.

"Tyson!" she cried, panic nearly choking her words. "Where are you?"

Her father caught her at the bottom of the stairs. "What is it? Where's Tyson?"

Laurel's heart was thundering painfully in her chest. "Tell me you put Tator Tot on the trailer?" She stumbled to check the pony's empty stall.

Her father was questioning the grooms in rapid-fire Spanish. Both shook their heads and Laurel suddenly felt very cold. She flew across the yard and nearly ran into Bryce as she tore through her parents' house. "Is Tyson here?"

"He's not in the loft?" Bryce asked.

"No! Oh, God, Bryce," she cried. "I think he's out there somewhere."

She ran back out of the house, her ears roaring and her mind numb. Black smoke was billowing in from the west. The stable yard was awash with firemen from the Glacier Creek fire department.

"Tyson!" she screamed as tears streamed down her face.

Strong arms wrapped around her and she breathed the familiar scent of Sam. He turned her to face him but she tried to pull away. She had to find her son.

"Laurel," he shouted above the noise.

Sam gripped her upper arms and gave her a shake. When she stopped struggling, he relaxed his hold and tipped her chin up with his finger so her eyes met his. That calm competence she so loved about him was reflected back at her. Despite the pandemonium in the stable yard, she suddenly felt as if they were the only two people in the world.

"I'm here," he said. His voice soothed her. "Take a deep breath."

She blew out a breath that sounded more like a sob.

"Good girl. Now take another one." His fingers were massaging her shoulders. "Now slowly, I want you to tell me what's wrong."

"I can't find Tyson. Or Oreo. Or Tator Tot." Despite his efforts to sooth her, Laurel's words were punctuated with gasps.

"When and where was the last place you saw him?"

"Last night. In his bed. I looked in on him about midnight."

"Where the hell could he be?" Bryce asked from behind her.

Sam's eyes never broke contact with hers. The compassion she'd seen that night in The Drop Zone was back. "We're going to find him, Laurel. I need you to tell me if he said anything unusual last night."

"He said he had a plan," she choked out.

"A plan?"

"Yes! We were talking about Bryce's wedding. He said he had a plan." Laurel nearly crumpled to the ground. "I didn't ask him what it was though," she sobbed.

"Laurel," Sam was using his captain's voice. "I need you to stay with me here. Is there somewhere he might go to hide? Somewhere on the ranch?"

"He has a fort," her father said. "Out toward the lake. It's an old abandoned storage shed."

"How do I get there?" Sam demanded.

Her father swallowed harshly beside her. "It'll be on the other side of the fire line."

"Holy shit," Bryce murmured.

She grabbed at Sam's fire suit. "Sam, please. You have to go get him. Bring him back to me."

He leaned in and kissed her on the forehead. "I told you,

Laurel, whatever you need from me."

And then he was shouting something at Liam about taking a crew and digging a line. The fire chief sought his guidance on where to position the hoses so that they could wet down everything between the fire and the buildings. He barked into his radio at Miranda to bring the helicopter to the ranch. Sam was a model of efficiency; a natural born leader. He continued giving orders and bringing organization to the chaos all the while holding Laurel's hand. Her father reached for her, but Laurel clung to Sam, refusing to let go. If anyone was going to find Tyson and bring him home, Sam would.

Five minutes later, Miranda was landing the helicopter in the south field. Sam made a motion like he was going to hand Laurel off to her father.

"No!" she cried. "I'm going with you."

Sam got that steely look in his eyes. "Not gonna happen, Laurel. You're a civilian. I can't take you into a fire."

She was behaving irrationally and impulsively, but she just didn't care anymore. "You and Tyson are the two people I love most in this world. If you're both going to be on the other side of this fire, you're not leaving me behind. You can't run away from this anymore, Sam. You can't run away from me. Now take me to get my son."

He swore savagely, but Laurel held her ground. "I swear I ought to have your father tie you up."

"The wind could shift at any minute," she cried. "We

have to get Tyson."

"Damn it." He dragged her the hundred yards to the helicopter. Miranda gave her a wide-eyed look as Sam lifted her into the chopper and handed her a headset.

"You'd better strap her in tight, Cap," Miranda said through the headset. "She's afraid of heights."

Laurel gripped Sam's hand tightly. "I'll be fine," she told her cousin. "Let's just hurry and get Tyson."

Miranda flicked a switch and suddenly they were going up.

MIRANDA SURREPTITIOUSLY TURNED off Laurel's headset and addressed Sam.

"The wind's shifting. The fire could change direction rapidly. We're going to have to get in and get out quickly."

"Ten-four," Sam said. The noise of the rotor was loud enough to drown out his words so Laurel couldn't hear their conversation. "I'm going to need you to keep her here."

Miranda snorted into her mouth piece. "She's a lot like her mother with that iron will of hers."

Sam looked down at their fingers. Laurel had both her hands wrapped around his left one in a death grip. She was breathing deeply through her mouth as she peered down at the fire below. Sam had been awakened at five-thirty this morning with a call from the base that a team was needed to fight a fire sparked by lightning near Whitefish. Kingston had taken a crew out while Sam made his way to the forest service station. He'd been monitoring other fires in the region when the call came in from Whispering Breeze. Sam told himself it was concern for Tabitha that had him jumping in his truck and racing to the ranch. But he knew it was Laurel and her family he was worried about.

When he'd arrived and seen her so distraught, he had only one singular concern and that was to take care of Laurel. To right whatever was wrong. He didn't give a thought to the fire or his crew. Hell, he'd even let her come on a mission with him. Sam would lose his job for sure. But when she'd told him she loved him, he couldn't bear to leave her behind. *Screw the job.* The only thing of importance right now was finding Tyson and getting both him and Laurel safely home.

Laurel squeezed his hand. "There," she mouthed at him. She pointed to a small red shed about two hundred feet from the lake.

Miranda switched Laurel's microphone back on. "It that big enough for the pony?" Miranda asked.

"It would be tight, but Tyson would want all the animals to be together," Laurel replied.

The chopper hovered next to the shed. Smoke from the fire had begun to billow back in their direction, lowering the visibility. Laurel reached for her seatbelt, but Sam grabbed her hand.

"I need you to stay put, Laurel. You wanted to come

along, but I'm in charge," he told her. "I'll go get Tyson and bring him to you."

She opened her mouth to protest, but Sam leaned into kiss her instead. "I'll be right back."

He pushed open the door and jumped on the landing skid before leaping to the ground. Covering his mouth to keep from inhaling the thick smoke, he ran to the shed.

"Tyson!" Sam called. "Are you in there?"

"Captain! I'm here!"

Sam gave the thumbs up sign to the women in the chopper. He tried to shove the door open, but it had been bolted from the inside.

"Tyson, open the door."

"I can't," Tyson cried. "Tots is scared of the fire and he'll bolt if I open it."

Swearing, Sam braced himself to catch two hundred pounds of amped-up miniature pony. "I won't let him get away. Open up, Sport."

Tyson cracked the door and Sam slid inside. The pony's eyes were wild, but fortunately Tator Tot was frozen in the corner of the room. Oreo yipped excitedly. Tyson jumped into Sam's arms.

"I'm sorry," he said, burying his face in Sam's neck.

Sam could hear the fire in the distance. He scooped up Oreo so he could make a run for the chopper. "What are you doing out here, Sport?"

Tyson sniffled next to Sam's ear. "I wanted to run away.

To make Daddy mad. But then the fire came and I got scared. I couldn't get back home."

Glancing through a crack in the door, Sam assessed the direction of the smoke. He continued to ask questions of Tyson in order to distract him from the scene awaiting them outside the shed. "Why did you want to make your father mad, Tyson?"

"Because he's marrying Audrianna. And he's not going to come live with us."

"Cap," Miranda called over the radio. "We need to expedite."

Sam hugged the little boy tighter, preparing to run. "Tyson, you and I are going to have to save this man-to-man talk for later."

"I can't leave Tots!"

"He won't fit in the chopper, Tyson." Sam looked over at the frightened pony. "I'll make sure he's safe. I promise."

"I get to ride in a helicopter?"

"Don't get too excited. Your mom is waiting in there for you."

Sam pulled the boy's jacket over Tyson and Oreo's noses before slipping out the door. The wind had shifted and the flames were now seventy-five yards from the shed. He ran through the thick smoke to the chopper and pulled open the door.

"Tyson!" Laurel cried when Sam tossed the boy and his dog inside.

"Mama!" Tyson jumped into his mother's lap and buried his head against her shoulder.

"Thank you!" Laurel called to Sam over the whirring of the chopper blade.

He nodded before grabbing two shovels and a respirator from the gear stowed in the back. "Get them out of here," he called to Miranda.

"No!" Laurel cried. "We're not leaving you here!"

"Damn it, Laurel, you can't tell me you love me then not trust me to do my job! Take Tyson home and wait for me there. I can handle this."

"He's gotta save, Tots, Mama. He promised."

Tears were streaming down Laurel's face. "I do love you, you know."

"I love you, too," Sam said without hesitation.

She grinned broadly as she swiped at her tears and Sam wanted nothing more than to kiss her.

"Cap," Miranda called from the cockpit. She gestured at the flames licking closer.

"Tator Tot and I will see you back at the ranch." Sam closed the door and gave it a slap with his palm, indicating to Miranda that she should take off.

Sam pulled his respirator over his face and began digging a fire line. The wind had shifted again, giving him room to work. But he needed to get the line dug as quickly as possible just in case the wind shifted back. Two minutes later, an ATV came hurtling across the pasture from the west. Dex

McCoy, one of the rookie recruits, and Molly Rivers jumped off and began digging a line on either side of him.

They worked in silence for the next thirty minutes, each of them competent at the task, until they'd made a line across the two acres. With no fuel on either side, the fire was beginning to burn itself out. Sam looked at his two crew members. "Nicely done."

McCoy looked behind him. "I had a little bit more incentive than usual. That's my family's property on the other side."

Sam let his mind wander to Laurel and Tyson. He'd had more motivation than normal for getting this fire out, too. He was in love with Laurel. And her son. Putting his heart out there again was a risk, but Sam knew now that it was one he had to take. He'd deal with her reservations about his career somehow. Even if it meant he had to make sacrifices. Sam realized his love for Becky hadn't been as deep as the love he now felt for Laurel. Their marriage had been doomed from the start despite both their best intentions. He hadn't failed Becky. They'd simply married for the wrong reasons. Sam had a second chance with Laurel, and he was going to do everything in his power to make it work.

"Glacier-one to Captain Gaskill." Jacqui Edwards' voice came over the radio in Sam's pocket.

He mentally shifted gears back to his job. "Go ahead, Jacqui."

"The incident coordinator of the Whitefish fire has lost

radio contact with Vin." Jacqui's voice broke as she spoke the words. "The rest of the crew has been unable to locate him."

Sam's gut clenched. Everyone on the crew carried a radio just for these circumstances. Best case scenario, Kingston's radio was malfunctioning. Sam didn't want to even consider the worst case scenario. Unfortunately, it sounded like Jacqui Edwards already had.

He'd suspected something was up between Jacqui and Kingston for weeks now. Both were discreet and professional while on duty, so Sam had looked the other way. A part of him had been happy the young widow had found comfort with a solid man like Kingston. He only hoped for everyone's sake that history wasn't repeating itself.

"Sit tight, Jacqui," he said into the radio. "Miranda and I will bring the chopper back to the base. We'll head out to Whitefish right away."

McCoy and Rivers' faces were solemn as they stared at Sam.

"We'll find him," Sam reassured them. "In the meantime, there's a frightened pony in that shed. I promised Tyson I'd bring him home. How are you with horses, McCoy?"

"Tator Tot and I are old friends, Cap. He's as much of a Houdini as Tyson is," McCoy said with a laugh. "I'll get him back to Whispering Breeze. You just concentrate on bringing Kingston home."

"THANKS FOR STAYING through bedtime," Laurel said as she slid the door to Tyson's bedroom closed. "We probably should have both sat down with him together initially. Then things wouldn't have gotten this far."

"I get why you wanted me to tell him. I'm sorry I tried to stick you with delivering news that would upset him." Bryce dragged his fingers through his hair. "This whole parenting thing is about as tricky as executing an Ollie for the first time." He looked over at Laurel. "You're really good at it, though. He and I are both lucky to have you."

She laughed. "Thanks. I think."

"I'm serious. Tyson is a great kid and it's because of you. I know it hasn't been easy. *I* haven't made it easy. But if they gave out gold medals for best moms, you'd get one for sure." Bryce reached down and picked up her sketchbook. A pencil sketch of Sam was staring back at him. "Soldier Sam is a pretty decent role model for a boy to have, too."

Laurel snatched the sketchbook away. "It's a little early in our relationship, Bryce. I don't think Sam and I are to that point yet."

"Aren't you? He seems very into you. And I don't remember you ever looking at me like the way you look at him."

She sank down on the sofa, not wanting to have this conversation with Bryce Johnson, the ultimate adrenaline junkie. He thrived on danger. He wouldn't understand her fears.

Bryce crossed his arms over his chest. "How many times do I have to tell you this, Laurel? You can be a great mom to Tyson and still have a life of your own. Sam seems like a standup guy. One who will stick it out for the long run. And he already knows if he treats you poorly, he'll have to answer to me. Out with it, Laurel. What's holding you back?"

Laurel would have laughed at Bryce's protectiveness except something in his words rang true. She was holding back. Despite telling Sam she loved him earlier, she was still frightened of moving toward a future with him.

"It's just—his job," she whispered. "I don't know how I'll live with the risk day in and day out."

"Love is a risk. One of you could die in a car accident or get cancer. Are you going to avoid any kind of romantic commitment because you're afraid of the risk?"

Flabbergasted, Laurel stared up at Bryce. "When did you become the love philosopher?"

He shrugged. "I guess I just live my life a little looser than you do. You should try it sometime." Bryce reached down and tugged her off the sofa. "Come on. Walk me out. Audrianna wants to see herself on *TMZ*. Did you know she almost died in a fire today?" He winked at her.

"Did you know I flew in a helicopter today?"

Bryce laughed as he draped his arm over her shoulder and led her down the stairs to the barn. "See that? You're loosening up already."

Laurel swallowed her laugh when she spied Sam standing

at the bottom of the stairs. His hair was damp and his face was stoic. He had his hands shoved deep inside the pockets of his faded jeans. Laurel breathed a relieved sigh at the sight of him.

Bryce squeezed her shoulders. "I believe this is where I cut out." He kissed Laurel on the cheek with a little more affection than was necessary. "If you have to tie Tyson to the bed to keep him there, do it."

She rolled her eyes, less at his joke but more at his attempt to make Sam jealous.

He took the last two steps and extended his hand to Sam. "Captain, I can't thank you enough for what you did today. You're certainly worthy of the hero worship Tyson bestows on you."

Laurel held her breath, but Sam didn't hesitate to take Bryce's hand. "I did what any other guy with my training would have done."

"Yeah, but you did it better. And I'm grateful you were around." Bryce glanced over his shoulder at Laurel. "Don't let her scare you off. She deserves a guy like you." He clapped Sam on the shoulder and wandered out of the barn.

The quiet settled around them as Sam's amber gaze seemed to swallow her whole.

"Vin?" she asked anxiously.

Sam nodded. "He rolled his ankle and fell into a ravine. Miranda long lined him out. He'll be good as new once his ankle heals."

Laurel collapsed down on the steps with a relieved sigh. "I'm so glad."

He leaned back against Tabitha's stall. "Mm. So is Jacqui Edwards."

"Wow." A surprised laugh escaped her lips. "I sensed they were close, but I didn't see that coming." She met Sam's eyes and suddenly her chest felt lighter. If Jacqui Edwards was willing to risk her heart with another smokejumper, why couldn't Laurel?

Are you going to avoid any kind of romantic commitment because you're afraid of the risk? Bryce's words bounced around in her head. *Take a chance,* her rash alter-ego shouted.

"Did you mean it when you said you loved me?" she whispered. She'd been on pins and needles all day wondering if he'd only said the words to placate her, when he wanted her to leave the fire.

"I did." He swallowed roughly. "I know we've both had relationships that didn't turn out the way we wanted. And there's the whole fear factor involved with my job. But we can make this work. You and me. Together. You just have to trust your impetuous nature. Because that impulsive Laurel is the woman I fell in love with."

Tears burned the back of her eyes and she couldn't seem to catch her breath. Up until this moment, she hadn't realized how desperately she wanted Sam to say those words.

Sam spread his arms wide. "Come here."

She leapt into his embrace and his mouth fused with hers in a deep, drugging kiss.

"I want this, Sam," she said when they'd both come up for air. "Whatever this is, I want it with you. Forever."

"That's good. Because after today, I'm pretty sure I can't live without you or Tyson."

And then he was kissing her again and Laurel didn't want him to stop. Ever. She threaded her hands into his hair and pulled him in closer. A moan escaped the back of her throat before Tabitha's snort startled them apart.

"Did my horse just tell us to get a room?" he asked with a laugh.

Laurel linked her fingers with Sam's and tugged him toward the stairs. "She's very cheeky that horse of yours."

Sam smiled at the mare. "I'd say she's just happy with her new home." He turned his panty-melting grin toward Laurel. "We both are." He followed her upstairs and proceeded to show her exactly how happy he was.

EPILOGUE

Four months later

"LADIES AND GENTLEMEN, welcome to the Ohio Expo Center. Home of the American Quarter Horse Congress," a voice boomed over the loudspeaker.

The butterflies were having a field day in Laurel's stomach. "You'd think I'd never done this before."

Her mother laughed. She sat in her wheelchair just outside the temporary stall housing Tabitha at one end of the convention center. Horse people and fans streamed past her mother wishing her well.

Jo Keenan had been the biggest human interest story of the two week competition. No one expected her mother to return to the western reining world's biggest stage, but she had. And in the preliminary rounds Laurel and Tabitha had proven themselves the pair to beat.

"You're allowed to be keyed up. It's been ten years since your last championship," her mother said. "A lot has changed since then. Except for your capabilities. You're a better rider today then you were then, even with a decade off. It's truly amazing."

A lot had changed, Laurel thought to herself as she sprayed show sheen on Tabitha's haunches. She glanced at the diamond ring on her left hand. Sam had slid it on her finger last night, joking that she needed a little more bling to go with the rhinestones in her competition shirt. And then he'd made love to her slowly and reverently, promising to worship her forever if she'd agree to marry him. Laurel blushed just thinking about how her body reacted to his, even after all these weeks.

She and Sam had survived the fire season. Sam had also helped her survive an even worse period—Tyson's two week vacation with Bryce and Audrianna. As for Tyson, he'd survived matriculating from Ivy's kindergarten class to first grade. He was quickly figuring out that having two sets of loving parents, while not the norm, definitely had its advantages and he happily accepted Audrianna and Sam into his life.

Laurel had passed the CPA exam on the first try, surprising even herself. Unfortunately, however, Rusty didn't make her the chief accountant. Not that Laurel was actually disappointed because it turned out Rusty would rather be a patron for Laurel's artwork than have her oversee his books. He set up a gallery for her next to the mint farm's gift shop and Laurel was making a name for herself in the region.

She patted Tabitha's neck affectionately. A lot had definitely changed. Suddenly, Laurel had a life that was better than any she'd dreamt of as an impetuous teenager.

"Mama!"

Laurel turned toward the door of the makeshift stall. Tyson stood in the aisleway, his face obscured by his cowboy hat and a billowing stick of pink cotton candy. "Look what Grandpa bought me!"

"Oh, Wayne, you'll give the boy cavities," her mother said as Tyson scrambled onto her lap.

With a sheepish look on his face, her father slipped into the stall and began to bridle Tabitha. "It's a special occasion. Besides, Sam said it was okay."

Laurel arched an eyebrow at her fiancé who was leaning a broad shoulder against the metal stall frame and looking sexy enough that she'd forgive him just about anything. She stretched up onto her toes and gave him a quick kiss, tasting cotton candy on his tongue.

"Mm, it seems both my boys have a sweet tooth." She reached for her hat and gently positioned it over hair that resembled plastic after her mother had applied a half can of Aqua Net to her head.

Sam adjusted the brim. "Nah, we're just both sweet on you."

Tabitha stomped a foot, impatient to leave the stall now that she was saddled.

"I hear you girl," her father said as he pulled the reins over the mare's head and began to lead her out. "Let's get this show on the road."

"Come on, Mama," Tyson called from his grandmother's lap as she wheeled her chair toward the ring. "It's almost your turn."

Laurel went to step out of the stall, but Sam blocked her path with his arm. "Wait," he said softly. He bent down to peer beneath her hat. "Thank you for doing this. This was important to Becky." Sam paused to clear his throat. "I failed her in so many ways, but I didn't want to fail her in this. I don't expect you to understand, but I wanted you to know that I love you for helping me see this through."

She reached up and brushed her fingers along his jaw, loving the feel of his skin beneath her fingertips. "You're a silly man, Captain Cowboy. Without Tabitha, I wouldn't have found you."

He wrapped his hand around hers and brought her fingers to his lips. "You'll always have me, Laurel."

"I hope so," she said around the lump that had formed in her throat. "Because I have some really big plans for you tonight after I win this thing."

Sam pulled her in for a kiss that was a hungry promise for the future. Their future.

"I told you they'd be kissing again, Grandpa!" Tyson tugged at her belt. "Come on, Mama. We haven't got all day."

She exchanged smiles with Sam. "Actually, Tyson, we have a whole lifetime. But right now we have a world title to win."

Laurel grabbed each of their hands and headed off to the ring to do just that.

The End

The Firefighters of Montana

Book 1: Smolder by Tracy Solheim

Book 2: Scorch by Dani Collins

Book 3: Ignite by Nicole Helm

Book 4: Heat by Karen Foley

Book 5: Flame by Victoria Purman

Available at your favorite online retailer!

About the Author

Tracy Solheim is the international bestselling author of the Out of Bound Series for Penguin. Her books feature members of the fictitious Baltimore Blaze football team and the women who love them. In a previous life, Tracy wrote best sellers for Congress and was a freelance journalist for regional and national magazines. She's a military brat who now makes her home in Johns Creek, Georgia, with her husband, their two children, a pesky Labrador retriever puppy and a horse named after her first novel.

See what she's up to at tracysolheim.com. Or on facebook at Tracy Solheim Books and Twitter at @TracyKSolheim

Thank you for reading

Smolder

If you enjoyed this book, you can find more from all our great authors at TulePublishing.com, or from your favorite online retailer.

TULE
PUBLISHING